Praise for
Howls of the Forgotten

"As I began reading the first chapter, I found myself being drawn in to experience what the author had laid before me."

Helen Lehman

"In reading Linda's book, Howls of the Forgotten, *I have been truly touched by the importance and value of relationships. This is a story of real life and is full of emotions and suspense. The reader will be motivated to read on to The very end. "*

Phyllis Huxley

Howls

of the

Forgotten

LINDA BONDY

HOWLS OF THE FORGOTTEN

Published by Linda Bondy, Edmonton, Canada

ISBN:
      Paperback   978-1-77354-456-4
         ebook   978-1-77354-457-1

Publication assistance by

PUBLISHING
PageMaster.ca

ACKNOWLEDGEMENTS

I thank Jesus for guiding me as I wrote this story.

I wish my Dad had lived to see me finish this story because he was the first to tell me to write it. Considering Dad was a writer himself, my respect for him got me started.

I thank my niece, Karen Ceraldi, who put together the book's cover picture.

Thank you also to my friends and family for their support and encouragement

Contents

PREFACE

I love living in the country because the birds and sounds of wildlife are easy to see, hear and enjoy, so I moved out to an acreage about 60 km northwest of Edmonton in 1983; at that time, only five other homes were in the area. With only a few humans, wild animals, big and small, would venture closer than they do now. Hearing coyotes howls at night was a symphony to my ears.

The area is populated now, so I only see the occasional moose, deer, marmot, and fox.

I've always been fascinated with wolves. My husband and I went to a wolf sanctuary in Golden B.C. to see them up close. We arranged to walk with a couple of the wolves and their handlers. One wolf the sanctuary raised from a pup was about ten months old and friendly. This beautiful young wolf jumped up between my husband and me, placing her paws on my shoulder and my husband's. What a thrill!

Before retirement, I worked downtown, and as I traveled there and on my lunch-hour walks, I saw many sad sights. I began to recognize some of the poor people that frequented the area; there were many. One young fellow walked with his head down most of the time, and his body language portrayed a life of rejection and abuse. I met him face to face on the street one day; I could see the hopelessness he felt in his eyes. Then, there was a thin woman who always had bruises on her arms and sometimes her face. I had become very fond of these poor souls and wished I could help them somehow.

Another morning on my way to work, I saw a lost dog that broke my heart. I wished I could have stopped and helped her. I was expected at work, so I looked for her on the way home. As I drove on, I was sad and upset about the dog, and that sadness brought to mind the plight of those poor souls on the street. They, too, had been rejected and forgotten.

The dog I had seen that morning was a beautiful young German Shepherd pup, about eight months old. She was on the side of the road; when I drove near her, she stepped out onto the road to see, I think, if I was her owner, the car behind me experienced the same thing. She was probably just another unwanted dog someone had abandoned in the countryside and forgotten.

Some people do that; how could they? I will never understand.

After work, I drove out of the city and began looking for her in case she had moved on. Nearing the place I'd seen her last, I was shocked to see the dog dead on the side of the road; someone either didn't see her or didn't bother to drive around the animal. That day I vowed to give that poor dog a life she was denied by writing a story about her; I would make that dog a German Shepherd and wolf cross to give her strength and country smarts. I call her Sabean.

I began to work on the outline for the story, and it occurred to me that it would also allow me to bring attention to the plight of the abused and poor. This story is about "need and rescue."

CHAPTER ONE

The Rocky Hill Wolf Pack

Psalm 104:10-12

He sends the springs into the valleys,
which run among the hills.

They give drink to every beast of the field: the wild asses
quench their thirst. By them shall the fowls of the heaven
have their habitation, which sings among the branches.

Canadian geese honked to one another in the sunny sky above as they returned to Alberta. A young buck nibbled at the new shoots of greenery while a squirrel watched him from a nearby tree. All at once, the buck's head came up, displaying lovely antlers and alert eyes. His ears turned to listen intently, then, in an instant, he bolted. The squirrel was venturing down the tree but scurried back up when the buck took flight. After a short time, the squirrel saw the danger; wolves were coming.

Indeed, they were a wondrous sight, running together, everyone knowing their place in the pack. Obedience and harmony made them who they were, a dangerous force to be respected. The Park Ranger called them the Rocky Hill Pack.

They reached their pack site as the sun rose. Finding the perfect spot to lie down, they rested from their night hunt for the day.

The evening came, and the moon shone brightly. The wolves started to stir. Growler, the alpha male, stood up first. He stretched, shook his head, mounted a hill nearby, and began to howl loudly. Growler often howled on his own as if to remind the forgotten ones where they came from. He remembered those offspring who chose to leave to find a mate and start their own pack. Now the pack had forgotten them, except for Growler and his mate Breeze. Growler's ears perked up. He could hear a faint howl coming from the west. Soon the whole pack joined him in a short wolf song that died down quickly. Growler started running east, as did the others. Their territory extended northeast around a hundred km. and southwest about thirty-five km. They hunted mainly in the northeast. The pack would go to Huckle Lake in the west when the suckerfish were spawning. Too much further west, the wolves would run into humans, other wolf packs, and dangerous wildlife.

Growler's fur is black. When he lay down, his black coat appeared almost midnight blue. He was the largest of the pack and highly respected by the rest of the wolves. Growler's grandfather, Stormy, was mainly black, except for white under his neck and chest. Growler's mother, Maude, is predominantly silver and grey.

Maude was getting old, but the pack took excellent care of her, as is the custom of this wolf pack. She gave Breeze a break ever so often by looking after the pups. In her day, Maude was the alpha female. She sported a lovely thick, grey-to-silver coat. Her mate was killed on the highway by a car. Soon after Stormy's death, Growler took command of the other wolves.

Growler's mate, Breeze, is a beautiful female with a lovely grey and white coat. Her face is white to just above her eyes, and then grey dominates the rest of her body.

The other adults are Troy, who is second in command, and took on the colors of Stormy. Then there is Blaze, who is primarily grey and white; Sam is all black, and Ted is a mixture of gray and black.

Their territory this year was abundant with prey. The wolves frequented many small lakes; Black Spook Lake was one of their favorites. They enjoyed the cold water, and sometimes an unsuspecting animal seeking the same cold drink might become available. The wolves drank their fill. No volunteers turned up to catch, so the pack left. The cold, wet wind blew over the wolves for most of the night. Winter fur hung in lumps at their sides like old worn-out blankets.

It was time to hunt. Wolf silhouettes stood out against the hills as they mounted a steep one. The smell of far-off prey enticed them into a trot. They forged on until they caught up to the herd, and a young deer became their point of interest.

Growler started the chase with Troy close behind. Blaze veered off to the left of the herd while Sam and Ted took to the right. Growler's full potential burst through with Troy right beside him. Troy threw himself to the right of the young deer's hooves. He tried to grab the deer's leg, but she turned and managed to kick Troy hard in the shoulder, causing him to cry out in pain, which startled Growler and made him stop, that brief moment of hesitation allowed the young deer to get away and join the herd.

The yearling wolves were seven months old and were allowed to run with the pack. They were little to no help catching prey yet, but they were learning fast and gave another four sets of ears and eyes to detect prey or danger. The yearlings are mixed colors; Tembah is big and black, like his father. Teebo's coat is black, with white paws and chest. Tucker is a rugged-looking black and grey yearling with a black lightning bolt mark running down one side of his grey face. Haddie is predominantly white, a throwback to a relative named Chum.

Troy was limping when the rest of the pack gathered. His shoulder hurt, but he kept up with the others back to their pack site.

The sun was starting to rise in the eastern sky. They came to a gorge near the highway, where they found a young deer limping painfully from being hit by a truck.

The pack closed in on the poor creature, and soon her pain was over. The deer's death was quick. She would not have to face a cruel, cold, and hungry winter, which would have made the deer's inevitable death slow and excruciating. Growler attached himself to the animal first. Troy limped to the other side. Sam, Ted, and Blaze found a spot. The yearlings moved in to get their portions while avoiding the older wolves. They ate until they were full, then returned to the den sight, carrying meat for old Maude and Breeze.

Sounds of whimpering from inside the den broke the early morning silence. Breeze was nursing her pups. The den was up a small hill a few yards from the pack site.

Breeze is a dedicated mother. She has given birth to six healthy pups, four girls and two boys. The females looked like their mother, while the males took on Growler and Stormy's colors.

The smell of meat became evident. Breeze's ears stood straight up, and she poked her head out of her den. She found the food Growler had brought her, grabbed it, and hungrily ate, then lay down with her babies. The pups were still blind and deaf but knew their mother's smell. The largest male pup was Duke, who muscled his way among the other pups to get to his mother's milk first. The other little ones, Opie, Lacey, Europa, Casey, and Rascal, joined Duke and began eagerly sucking their mother's nourishing milk. Duke drank his full, then snuggled close to his mother and fell asleep.

Tired from hunting all night, the pack sat down and licked themselves clean. Troy's shoulder was bruised where the deer kicked him, but he didn't suffer any broken bones. He licked his painful shoulder.

Growler sat upon a hill. He just stared into the morning light as if expecting to hear something. His face seemed to become tighter, his wise dark eyes looked off into the distance, and his ears stood up as he could hear the howls of the forgotten in the northwest.

Still energized from the night's hunt, a couple of yearlings raised their heads and howled. Soon the rest of the pack joined in. It was a good time in a wolf's life.

Two young wolves, Haddie and Teebo, tumbled around as they played. Tembah sat and watched his siblings. Tucker joined in the fun. Soon they ran off into the bush; rustling twigs and yips were all you could hear. As they ran back, one could see only their happy faces as they made their way through the wild brush before settling down. It wasn't long before they were all enjoying a nap.

Breeze and her babies cuddled together and rested. She enjoyed having puppies next to her again. She was a loving mother, and her puppies were healthy. Contented, Breeze fell into a well-deserved sleep.

CHAPTER TWO

Joyce, Michael, Paul & Sabean

Last year's leaves lined with frost flew like dark specters as they passed in front of the full moon. It was an unusually windy April evening in Bently, Alberta. A red-cheeked girl bundled in a warm, black coat hurried along the sidewalk in front of Paul Ross' home.

In Ross's backyard, a lonely wolf/German Shepherd cross lay under a large evergreen tree. Her name is Sabean, and she is about eleven months old. A thick chain surrounded her neck, then led to the tree trunk where it wrapped around; she had only eight feet of freedom.

The wolfdog raised her head, and her ears perked up for full sound recovery. She could hear wolves howling in the distance from the northeast. The young wolf cross listened to her half-cousins for several minutes. She returned the call, but the sadness was evident in her long-drawn-out howl. The poor animal spent hours alone, chained to that tree. Her unbrushed coat was dirty, and winter fur lumps hung on her body. Sabean lives on a cup of cheap dog food daily and leftover scraps from the Ross table.

Sabean inherited her wild wolf father's muscular appearance. Her thick coat had some of her German

Shepherd colors, a tinge of reddish-brown fur on her ears and nose. Reddish brown mingled with dark brown fur continued down her back. Her copper-colored eyes showed acute alertness, but as she heard the far-off howls, they closed, and she laid back down with a deep moan. Sabean became so lonely that she sometimes whimpered as she positioned her head between her paws. Several attempts at freeing herself from the neck chain that imprisoned her most of the time exposed a thick strip of missing neck fur.

Her ears perked up again. She could hear the door latch squeak as it turned, and to her delight, it was Michael, Paul Ross' son.

Michael wore tattered jeans and a white T-shirt that said in big letters, 'I Love Hockey.' He adjusted his worn ball cap and then sat down beside Sabean. He gave her a small plate of food scraps and watched her eagerly gulp it down. Michael felt sad for the wolfdog. He began petting her, then whispered in her ear.

"Your wolf cousins can hear you, girl, and know you're here," soothed Michael.

Mike gently scratched around the furless areas and up under her neck. Six-year-old Michael was a typical freckled face kid that stood about four feet high. His love for the wolfdog was apparent in his big green eyes. The young boy put his arms around the big animal and said he loved her. Rubbing Sabean's head, Michael unlatched the neck chain.

"I'll let you run around the yard, but only for a few minutes before dad gets home." Sabean ran like the wind around and around the yard, and then, at Michael's command, she returned to her chain. Mike regretfully put the chain collar back on the animal and said,

"The weekend is near, and dad is hardly ever home, so we'll have a great time then. Maybe we'll play ball, girl." Michael wrinkled his face and continued, "as long as dad isn't around."

He wiped his dirty blond hair away from his eyes, kissed Sabean, and continued petting her.

"Michael, come in now, dear," Joyce yelled. The child ignored his mother's call and kept stroking the wolfdog.

"I've saved part of my sandwich for you, girl," Michael said as he handed the half-eaten peanut butter sandwich. Sabean gulped it down, and her tail wagged.

"Michael William Ross, you get in here now before your dad gets home!" Joyce warned.

The thought of his father made Michael grimace as he looked toward his mother.

"Michael, I don't want you to get in trouble with your dad," his mom explained.

Mike whispered to Sabean, "I'll come and see you before school in the morning, girl.

He gave Sabean a couple more strokes, then ran for the back door of his home.

Michael's home was an older trailer that needed repairs but sheltered the Ross family from the rain. Apparently, the trailer had very little insulation because the living room drapes would blow inward from the wall as the wind snuck through the metal siding. Mice had made homes in the walls, reducing insulation even more. When a thunderstorm was in full vigor, the pale blue siding flexed back and forth, adding to the booms that scared Michael. Mike would retreat under his bed covers if the storm landed at night. On the other hand, Joyce loved the wind, thunder, and heavy rain sounds. She appreciated the loose siding on the trailer as it made the sound of the storm even more exhilarating.

Joyce was a meticulous housekeeper and was constantly cleaning up mouse evidence. She tried her best to make her home presentable. The 14-foot wide by 64-foot-long trailer contained two bedrooms and one bathroom equipped with a stackable washer and dryer. Joyce's friend, Betty, and her husband, Jim, gave Joy a solid wood room divider, allowing her to separate the kitchen and living room areas.

Joyce, or Joy, as her friends called her, is a good-looking, slim lady with long wavy, auburn hair. She stands close to 6 feet tall and has lovely blue eyes.

She looked at her son lovingly, helped the boy take off his coat, kissed his cheek then said,

"You know, if dad had come home and seen you with Sabean off her leash, he'd surely hit you, then go out and probably kick that poor animal."

"Why doesn't he like Sabean anymore?" Michael asked with a pout.

"I think he just got tired of looking after her. The novelty of having a half-wolf dog has worn off. When he bought her, he thought it would be fun to have a big wolfdog, but now, he's too busy for her." Joyce confided.

Michael stood in the kitchen briefly, thinking he should tell his mom how he felt about his dad. Mike was afraid of his father, who often slapped him on the side of his head when Joyce wasn't watching.

Frowning slightly, Mike said, "Dad's always buying beer and stuff, and that's why we have nothing. My friend's dad takes him places and buys him things when he needs them."

"Now, quiet, don't say things like that about your father. I don't want you to dislike your dad," Joyce said softly.

"Dad works hard all week to pay the bills like food, electricity, and heat to keep us warm. He gives me money to buy the food we eat. I know he gets tired and grumpy. When you get tired, I've seen you grumpy too. Dad also has a bad knee that hurts him most of the time." Joyce paused and held Michael lovingly, "My dear Michael, you're best to just stay out of his way unless he wants you," Joyce warned.

"Just remember I'm always here for you, and Jesus is too," Joyce said with compassion written all over her face.

"But mom, dad is always mad at us for no good reason," Michael said, looking annoyed.

Joyce's face became solemn, then she said, "You should share your feelings with Jesus, and He'll comfort you. You pray to Jesus, don't you? If you want to get to know him, you must pray to Him, and he'll become your best friend."

Michael knew the face his mother portrayed when she brought Jesus into the equation.

"I don't really understand what praying is about," Mike said.

Joyce explained, "praying to God is simply talking to Him. Even though you can't see Him, He's always with us. That's how I get through life. However, you must approach God respectably. After all, He is the Creator, so always pray to God in the name of His son, Jesus."

Mike hugged his mother and said, "Mom, you always make me feel better."

She motioned Michael to the kitchen chair, and Joyce sat beside him and prayed a blessing over their meal. Mike dove into his supper, and that made Joyce very happy. Joy had only the basic spices that were on sale. She could see her boy was growing and how he enjoyed the food she had made for him. Meatloaf with mashed potatoes and gravy were one of the boy's favorites. He was hungry, and it didn't take long before he finished.

"Is there any dessert tonight, mom?" Michael asked, hoping.

"Yes, there is," Joyce said, then added, "I just got the apple pie out of the oven, so wait a bit, and you can have some when it cools down."

"Apple pie, what a treat. Can I go to my room until the pie cools?" Mike asked.

Joyce nodded, and the boy ran off, shutting his door behind him.

Mike was an obedient boy who respected and loved his mother; however, he didn't share those feelings with his father.

Michael busied himself until Joyce announced the pie was ready to be eaten. He ran into the kitchen, slid onto his seat at the table, and gobbled down a piece.

"Mom, you make the best pies in the whole world," Mike said with a big grin.

Joyce wiped the boy's face with a damp cloth, which Mike didn't like her doing, but his love for her allowed it.

After this invasion of his face, Mike went and played in his room for the evening.

It was Michael's bedtime, and Paul still hadn't gotten home.

Joyce said, "Time to get ready for bed, dear."

Michael washed up, brushed his teeth, and put on his PJs.

"Mom, I'm ready for bed," Mike said as he entered the kitchen. Joyce looked him over and kissed him. She hugged him and told him she loved him.

I love you too, mom," replied Mike, then he ran into his room and got into bed. Joyce followed him and prayed over her son, and Mike prayed too. Joyce kissed his head and said, "Goodnight."

Paul Ross is six foot two tall and quite muscular, except for his beer belly. His eyes are green, and his hair is dirty blond. He works at the sheet metal factory. It's good company. The pay is good, with a pension plan and life insurance in place. Paul was badly teased by his co-workers, who told him he'd be dumb not to contribute to the plans and to think of his family in case anything ever happened to him. He would have preferred to spend that money on himself but gave in to the ridicule and arranged to have money for the plans taken off his cheque.

As soon as Paul heard the sound of the end-day whistle, he would be on his way to the local bar. Paul would meet some of the men he worked with there. It never occurred to him to phone Joyce to tell her he'd be late. Paul was more interested in playing pool and drinking with the boys. The conversation was always the same, one would start complaining about the job, and the rest took turns doing the same.

It wasn't long before Paul felt the liquor and started a loud conversation with one of the guys; no one knew who was right, so things quieted down.

Paul never graduated from school due to laziness mainly. He wasn't the factory's star employee but managed to keep his job. The men started to disperse around 8:45 p.m., leaving Paul and another fellow at the table.

"Well, I guess I'd better go home too, so I'll see you tomorrow Roman," announced Paul. Roman is divorced and quite an alcoholic; he tipped his beer glass to indicate goodbye.

Around 9:15 p.m., Paul's rusted, blue truck rumbled to a stop in front of his mobile home. Paul stumbled out of the truck, caught his foot, and fell on the ground as he attempted to disembark. Getting back on his feet, Paul slammed the truck door shut. Staggering to his back door, he turned the doorknob and found it locked as per his rules. Fumbling for the key among the other six keys in his pocket angered Paul. Finally, finding the right key, he put it in the keyhole but dropped it on the ground. He yelled profanities loudly while he searched for it. Paul felt something, and the dark words he was spewing stopped. He turned the door handle, entered, slammed the door behind him, threw his coat on the floor, and headed for the kitchen.

Joyce! I'm home. Get me my supper." Paul demanded,

"I've kept your supper warm in the oven. I didn't think you would be so late." Joyce replied.

"That's your problem, Joyce, you never think." Paul grumbled as he sat down at the table, then slurred, "Get it for me!"

Joyce brought out the meatloaf from the oven. It had been warming for close to four hours. Grabbing a fork and knife, she placed the food in front of him.

"What's this slop, Joyce? It looks like garbage!" Paul yelled as he pushed the plate onto the floor, "Give it to that cur outside!" Paul barked.

He grabbed Joyce's hair as she knelt down to pick up the plate and food.

"Don't hurt me, Paul. I'm sorry. I'll make something fresh for you," Joyce pleaded.

"You can't seem to get anything right, you hag," Paul screamed directly in her ear, leaving a high-pitched ringing sound, causing Joyce pain for some time. Paul let go of her hair. Joyce continued cleaning the floor, and as she finished, she heard Paul snoring. He had fallen asleep in the kitchen chair. Joyce knew she would have to wake him so he could go to bed but feared getting grabbed again. Just then, Paul opened his eyes and stood up. He weaved his way to the bedroom and fell sideways on the bed. Joyce could see there wouldn't be any room left on the bed. She shut the bedroom door and went into Michael's room. He was asleep in his bed with his monster truck beside him. Joyce moved the truck to his night table and kissed him softly on his cheek. Michael's face looked peaceful, and she thought how nice it would be if he could feel that calm when he was around his dad. Paul's disposition didn't allow for much peace, and she could see Michael's body tense up every time his father was near him.

Paul had a quick temper and often took it out on Joyce and sometimes his son.

Joyce returned to the kitchen, did the dishes, and tidied up. Paul wouldn't stand for a messy house. It was routine for Joyce to sweep her floor at least two to three times daily. When washing the floors, she went on her hands and knees to do the job. Paul and Michael's clothes were always clean and ironed. She had to do a load of washing almost every second day because Michael, a typical boy, would come home with dirty clothes. Considering Mike and Joyce had only a few clothes, Joyce ensured the washing was current. As Joyce washed her sink, she quickly checked around to see how everything looked, entered the living room, and sat on their old, worn-out green couch.

There were times when she felt fed up and fought her inner need to fight back. Joyce was emotionally exhausted; closing her eyes, she said her prayers. Talking to Jesus always gave her comfort and peace. Joyce opened her eyes and took a soft brown quilt draped over the couch's back; wrapping the quilt around herself, she lay on the couch, curled her knees up, and quickly fell asleep.

CHAPTER THREE

Alfred Gilmore
and Friend, Bert

Winter had passed, but it was still very chilly on this late April day. A rather run-down house stood on the corner of Lions and Brook with the Gilmore family living inside.

"Alfred! get out of bed and get to school," Darlene yelled up the stairs to her son.

Alfred's mother's breath already smelt of liquor and cigarettes. Her face looked several years older than her 34 years. Darlene dressed in loose clothes that were short of being clean; her appearance told how she felt about herself and life. A bottle of cheap wine stood beside Darlene's couch most of the time, and a cigarette hung out of her mouth. The TV was her only entertainment and convenient because she wouldn't have to move from the comfort of her couch.

Alfred slowly threw off his covers and got out of bed. He was a side sleeper, so his thick, black hair stood straight up on one side of his head. Rubbing his eyes, Alfred thought of school and dreaded it.

He thought about the day before when the counselor called him to his office. Mr. Humphrey told Alfred he was borderline retarded, and should probably look at menial labor jobs when he leaves school. Alfred took this news hard. Alf thought his brother was right and that he was indeed stupid. Alf stuttered when he became excited or anxious, which didn't help when he spoke to the counselor.

As he put his clothes on, Alfred thought about his grandfather, who often quoted the Bible and told him many things about Jesus when he visited. The sadness on his face turned to a soft grin as he recited Proverbs 23:7, "For as a man thinks, so he is." Alfred thought he'd try to think positively and be happy today. His granddad taught him that Jesus loved him dearly, making his life bearable. Love didn't seem to exist in Alfred's home.

Darlene screamed at him to hurry up, "Okay, Ma, I'm com-coming." he replied.

Alfred's mother is a Cree Indian, and his father is an Englishman with a short temper. Alfred took his mother's darker skin but inherited his dad's thin stature.

Alfred, Al, Alf, or Alfie, as he was also known, walked most of the time with his head down from a lack of confidence in himself. He had just turned seventeen and was very shy.

Alf's brother, Larry, is just the opposite; he is nineteen, handsome, well-built, and tall. He has jet-black hair and light brown skin. Larry inherited his father's dark eyes, making him appear almost exotic. He got a kick out of teasing and pushing Alfred around, and this morning was no different.

Hey, loser, you better get your lazy self downstairs," Larry yelled.

"I'm coming!" answered Alfie as he put the last of his clothes on. He picked up some books for school and smiled because he remembered them this time. Alfred's teacher,

Mrs. Sandra Forbes, reminded him to bring his books to school daily. Sandra had a soft spot for Alfred and felt sorry that the kids picked on him terribly. Al liked his teacher and tried his best not to forget his books and pay attention in her math class. Mrs. Forbes's encouragement helped ensure that her students learned the world of numbers.

Oh, wow, look who remembered his books, and your head too," Larry laughed.

"I can't forget my head, Larry, because it is part of my body," Alfred grumbled.

Larry shook his head, rolled his eyes, then laughingly said, "Well, I see you have a few brain cells working at least."

Both brothers grabbed a couple of pieces of cold store-bought pizza from the kitchen table from the previous night's meal, one piece for breakfast and one for lunch. The fridge was usually empty except for wine and beer. Sometimes they would find bread, margarine, and peanut butter if their father thought about it. They didn't expect their mother to make breakfast or lunch, for that matter. Darlene seldom thought about anybody but herself.

Bert was the only friend Alfred had. His family is practicing Christians, as is Bert. Alfred became part of their family at a young age, and they treated him like one of their own. Occasionally Mrs. Black would give him some socks and gloves in the winter. Virginia Black, and Dave, her husband, could see Alfred was undernourished and would ensure he had something to eat when he visited. Virginia gave Alfie a nice pair of pants, and Al accepted it with sincere gratitude. Unfortunately, when Darlene noticed the new pants, she went into a rage and said that her family didn't accept charity. Darlene screamed at Alfred and told him to take them off and return them immediately. Poor Alf was so embarrassed when he returned the pants to Mrs. Black.

"That's okay, Alfred, don't be upset. I should have checked with your mom first, so it's my fault," Virginia soothed.

"Thank you, Mrs. Black, for understanding. My mom is a very proud woman," Al said.

The next day Bert was waiting for Alf outside his house. They walked and talked the five blocks to the school almost every morning.

Bert is a tall, skinny kid with a face full of freckles and thick curly brown hair. He likes playing video games, board games, and cards with Al. Bert met Alfred when they started grade one. The kids at school bullied Bert, forcing him to be alone until he noticed Al. The school kids tormented Alfred much worse than Bert. One day Bert took a chance and introduced himself to Al. They became good friends and have formed a deep bond over the years.

As they walked to school, Bert shouted, "Guess what, Al?"

"What?" Alfred pushed for the news.

"Okay, okay, I am getting my driver's license. I passed my learner's license already. Dad has been giving me lessons. He said that I was learning quickly. I hope to do my driver's test in a couple of weeks," Bert said proudly.

"And you didn't think to tell me, your best buddy," Al expressed, smiling.

"I had such a hard time not telling you. I started practicing and admit I was a bit scared at first and wasn't sure if I could learn. I didn't want you to think I was stupid.

Dad said I am learning fast and will let me drive to Topaz to take my driving test when the time comes." Bert relayed.

"That's fantastic, Bert. I'll be rooting for you, and I know you'll do fine," Al inspired.

The boys arrived at school, and Bert said, "Thanks, buddy. I have to go to the gym because I forgot my towel yesterday, so I'll see you later."

Bert ignored the insults the kids at the entrance to the school yelled.

"Hey, freckle freak! Oh, look! He's with stupid," one kid yelled.

Canby High is a tough school, and you would be an outcast if you didn't belong to a group. Alfred and Bert were perfect candidates for such a role.

Al moved through the school ground to a bench he liked to sit on at the side of the school. Some kids saw him and started teasing and being mean to him.

Alfie's hair stood up even though he'd combed it; it would spring back up, then sloped to one side like a plume. Some kids would laugh at him and call him Birdboy. Most of his clothes were Larry's hand-me-downs. Some of the older kids recognized the clothes and found them quite laughable.

"Hey, Birdboy, pull up your pants before you lose them," one kid shouted.

"It's hard enough looking at you without seeing any more of your disgusting body, Alfred!" Larry added.

Larry did odd jobs after school, which afforded him some nice clothes. He saw his friend George near the gym door and strutted over to him.

"Your brother should be somewhere where people don't have to look at him, Larry," George jeered.

"I agree with you, man, but what can a guy do?" Larry said, then laughed.

Since childhood, George and Larry had been friends, and neither cared very much for their siblings. Larry was embarrassed by Alfred.

Alf waited for the bell to ring. He noticed early spring flowers popping through the leftover snow. It was cool outside, but the sun shone brightly, making one feel warmer than they were. Alfred loved to daydream and often imagined living with his grandfather, Bill Dennis

The school bell rang loudly, making Alfred jump to a standing position. He headed to his class. Mrs. Forbes knew Alfred loved mathematics and caught on to everything she taught. Sandra had his full attention. Al especially loved geometry and found it fun and challenging. His next class was English, taught by Mr. Dixson. English didn't interest him, and instead of learning, Al daydreamed. Alfred knew in his heart that his granddad, his good friend Bert, and Bert's family were the only ones that cared for him, unlike his own family.

It was now Friday, and the school day was almost over. Finally, the bell sounded, and Alfred slowly walked out the door.

"Hey, stop! Let me catch up!" yelled Bert, "In the mood for a video game I just got?" Bert coaxed.

"Sure, sounds great," Al responded.

My mom wants to talk to me when I get home, so could you please play a game or two on your own while I'm with her?" Bert asked.

"No problem, buddy," Al replied.

When the boys got to Bert's, Al went into Bert's bedroom to play a game while his friend entered the living room, where his mom smiled as he entered.

"Sit down, dear," Virginia said as she patted the chair next to her and then continued, "Your dad and I have talked it over, and we feel if you continue to show us that you can be a safe driver, do all your chores, do well in school, and pass your driver's test, we would like to give you our van."

"You're going to give me the van?" Bert asked in disbelief.

"Dad needs a newer vehicle. We want to buy a small economical car. That old faithful van still has plenty of miles left on her. It's a gas eater but works well. You might consider taking on some jobs around the neighborhood for gas money. So, what do you say to that son?" Virginia announced.

"Mom, you can count on me to do my best in all your mentioned areas. I just can't believe it! How did I ever get such thoughtful parents like you guys? Thank you so much," Bert said with amazement in his voice and face.

"Dad will be taking you for a lesson tonight when he gets home," Virginia reminded him.

"Can Al sit in the back?" Bert pleaded.

"If it's okay with dad. I'm pretty sure he won't mind." Bert's mom surmised.

Bert kissed and hugged his mom, then dashed to join Alfred in his room.

"I have fantastic news!" Bert blurted.

"More good news?" Alf questioned.

Bert filled Al in on what his parents intended to do for him.

Bert remarked, "The van is in great shape but has some rust around the wheel wells. Mom and dad bought the van new and have always taken it to the dealership for any maintenance or repairs needed, so it should do me for a few years," Bert said with pride.

"Wow! Boy, you sure have great parents, Bert," Al stated.

"I know. I am very blessed indeed. If it's okay with dad, do you want to go with us for my driving practice when dad gets home?" Bert coached.

It didn't take any coaching because Alfie loved Bert's family and was happy for his friend. They waited for Bert's father, talking non-stop about his future van. Bert got set to play a video game with Al and warned, "Get ready to lose my friend."

Bert couldn't seem to win a game and complained, "Hey, that's the third game you've won, Alfie. Your reactions are so quick," Bert said with a playful pout.

"Thanks, buddy, not bad for a stupid person like me," Al remarked.

"Stop saying that, Alfred. Don't listen to your brother and those rotten kids at school. You could make something of yourself, given half a chance," Bert encouraged.

Alfred smiled at the compliment. Bert suggested they could someday drive up the highway and visit his granddad.

"I would love that! I'm dying for you to meet my granddad, Bert," replied Al.

They began another game when Mr. Black pulled into the driveway. Bert and Alf stood at the door to meet him. Dave jumped a bit when he opened the door to find the boys standing right before him.

"What's up, boys?" Dave speculated.

Bert's smile couldn't be any wider when he told his dad that he knew what they planned to give him if he lived up to their expectations.

"Yes, son, that's what we plan to do," Dave concurred.

"Thank you both with all my heart. Dad, can Al come with us for my driving lesson?" Bert asked, hoping.

"Well, okay, but it will have to be after supper. So, Alfred, would you like to stay for supper?" Dave asked.

"Would I? Wow, you bet I do," Al said gleefully.

Bert and Al finished the game they had started earlier when Virginia called them for dinner. Alfred didn't know where to start. There was roast pork, mashed potatoes, corn, and salad. Al filled his plate and tried to eat slowly, not to embarrass himself. He was so hungry, and each bite tasted good.

"Save room for blueberry pie and ice cream, boys," Virginia warned.

Al considered eating supper with Bert's family a luxury, and the homemade pie was divine. Bert and Al finished about the same time. Their contented faces pleased Mrs. Black.

"Thank you so much," Alf said as he rubbed his full tummy.

After dinner, the boys washed and dried the dishes and then sat with Bert's parents in the living room. They were ready to move to the van as soon as Mr. Black nodded.

"Well, fellows, ready for an evening drive?" Dave inquired.

Dave and Bert sat in the front seat, while Virginia and Alfred sat in the back. Poor Bert was nervous and hoped he would do well. Off they went, and Bert drove slowly, without error.

"Way to go, son. I must be a pretty good teacher, wouldn't you say, Alfred," Dave remarked.

"You sure are, and I can't believe how fast you're catching on, Bert." vocalized Alf.

"My son is a fast learner, and we're very proud of him," Virginia remarked.

They returned to Bert's. Bert informed Alfred they couldn't get together this weekend because he and the family plan to visit his grandmother in Whitewolf.

Okay then. I'll miss you, buddy," Alf said as he left.

Larry was happy about the weekend ahead. Al spent the day planning to visit his grandfather during the summer holidays.

CHAPTER FOUR

Bill Dennis

Alfred's granddad, Bill Dennis, is a Cree Indian and was nearly seventy-four years old. He is a thin but muscular man, around 5 foot nine, who has worked hard throughout his life. The hard work kept him in shape to live the lifestyle needed to survive in the bush.

He had given his life to Jesus a few years ago and learned to cast his cares upon the Lord. He believed Jesus would take care of him, and He did.

Bill had built a small but functional cabin and was proud of it. Although it wasn't much to look at, it is well built.

A picture of a young woman in a wooden frame sat beside the old guy's bed on his night table. That is the only picture he had of his lovely, departed wife. He treasured Helen's picture. She had died after giving birth to Alfred's mother, Darlene. Bill did his best to bring her up, but she was wild. She ended up pregnant with Larry when she was fifteen. Bill's daughter left home and didn't tell him where she was for almost three years. Darlene returned for a short visit and told Bill she had married Jake Gilmore, and they lived in Bently.

Bill went to visit her and his grandsons every couple of months. Alfred was always delighted to see him, but Larry didn't care one way or another. One day Bill stopped visiting; he was tired of seeing Darlene degrade herself with her heavy drinking. She would swear and yell. Bill couldn't take it anymore and cut his last visit short. He hugged young Alfred and then handed him a letter that contained a map of how to get to his grandfather's place.

Bill whispered in Al's ear, "Come and stay with me, Alfie, anytime you like."

He got his stuff together, gave Alfred another long hug, then said goodbye. Alfred cried and said he would be out to see him as soon as he could.

The elderly man went to the Bently Bank, where the government deposited his pension, and he withdrew enough money to buy supplies. While on his way home, Bill stopped to buy some dry goods. He had brought down a large, sturdy suitcase on big wheels to accommodate bulk food to take back home. The 'Everything Bulk' store had pasta, rice, powdered milk, flour, coffee, dehydrated vegetables, and dried meat. The grocery store allotted him some groceries, then at Jack's Snacks & Stuff, he bought a new camouflage jacket, matching cap, and a huge backpack, all on sale. They smelled heavily of Patchouli oil. Bill put the jacket and cap in his new backpack. As Bill stuffed the jacket, he thought of Alfred, grinned, and stuffed a second jacket and cap in for Alfred. It was the same size as Bill's, but he knew Al would grow into it.

Bill knew Alfred would come and visit him one day. Equipped with what he needed for a couple of months, he left for his cabin. When the old man was a bit younger, the thirty-four km walk home was no problem, but now hitch-hiking was easier. If no one picked him up, he would walk as far as he could, then find a place in the bush to rest for a while, and then carry on. Bill lives out in the bushy forest of Alberta near Whitewolf. He is a tough fellow and very independent. He lives mainly off the land as his father did before him. Bill considered himself a pretty good fix-it man and did any repairs required for the cabin and the two small sheds he had built. Placing his ball cap on, armed with a hammer and nails, he could just about fix or build anything.

Bill stopped on the road, pulled out the new camouflage cap, and exchanged it with the one on his head. He smiled at buying the new cap. He also liked the smell of his new gear.

Bill thought of Alfred and how he would miss him as he walked the rest of the way home. He arrived at his cabin in the late evening. After putting his supplies away, Bill was pretty tired. He poured some water into his washbasin and washed. Feeling clean, he changed into his pajamas, made some porridge, and sat at his little table. He was hungry and finished his meal quickly. The old bloke threw his wash water off his porch, where his potatoes grew. He replaced the dirty water with fresh water to soak his dinner pot, bowl, and spoon overnight. After finishing that, he climbed into bed.

Bill woke just before sunrise. He started a fire in his potbelly stove, went outside, and brought in more wood. Filling the stove, it wasn't long before Bill could put on a pot of coffee. Once brewed, old Bill went out on the porch with his coffee cup and sat in his rocking chair. He loved to watch the sun as it rose. He enjoyed the many birds singing while he planned his day.

The man walked out onto his land; he set up his traps now that he was back home. He disabled his traps whenever he had to leave for a while. Bill was not going to risk catching an animal only to starve it. He mainly caught small animals like rabbits, squirrels, and groundhogs for food. He lived on the same land most of his life, was well aware of the meat eater's territories, and kept to his land, but he didn't need to go far to find something to eat. Bill picked up a pail and picked enough of nature's herbs to throw into the stew he would make later. Most folks call what God provides weeds, but many are edible and good for the body. They taste pretty good, too, if you know how to cook them."

Bill dried many herbs in the late summer and fall for the winter. He would pour the dried herbs into large pickle jars a restaurant gave him years ago. The old fellow stored them under his bed and on a shelf over his headboard. Some plants are for eating, and others for healing. He used some to make tea and poultices. He depended on those dry herbs to make soup and add to stews. The old timer made teas for various ailments like colds or flu. The tea would either stop the ailment or shorten the sickness's duration.

Bill smiled and thought how wonderful the Lord was. He was constantly amazed at what God provided for free. The Lord sows different wild plants for different areas. Some places are prone to illnesses that require herbs that don't grow in Alberta. God sows the right plants for food and medicine everywhere in His world.

The sun was almost at high noon, and Bill's pail was full, so he returned to the cabin. He was hungry. The elderly man got on all fours near the door and removed a mat and loose flooring that revealed a fair-sized hole. Bill stepped into the hole that led under the cabin and the porch where Bill had built a root cellar. He opened the cellar door, stepped down a few steps, carefully made his way around a pile of potatoes on the floor to a wall of shelves, and pulled out a stew pot. His flashlight didn't give off good light, and as he walked back, he almost stumbled over his wooden sandbox that contained carrots. That cellar was handy when one didn't have electricity for a fridge. The cellar saved good food from spoiling and kept the perfect temperature for vegetables and anything he needed to keep cool but not freeze in the winter.

Bill was thankful he built the cellar. He built the cabin and porch over it when his father died, leaving him the land and his old home. Bill grew up in that home and raised Darlene, but it was in bad shape, so Bill tore part of it down and salvaged enough wood to build his cabin. It is considerably smaller than the old house but quicker to heat, and Bill loved his home.

CHAPTER FIVE

Back at the Pack

Job 12:7-10

"But ask the beasts, and they will teach you; the birds of the heavens and they will tell you; or the bushes of the earth, and they will teach you, and the fish of the sea will declare to you. Who among all these does not know that the hand of the Lord has done this? In his hand is the life of every living thing and the breath of all mankind.

Tucker and Teebo were still full of excess energy from the night hunt at the pack site. They began to playfight and enjoy themselves. Tembah was bored and began to use his sharp teeth to pull on a tree root. He loved to tug and dig holes, which seemed to be his primary source of entertainment. Tembah was entirely reserved toward his siblings and lorded over them. Haddie became interested in what Tembah was doing and made her way next to him. Although Tembah tolerated Haddie, she got a little too close, and he bared his teeth and growled a warning. Haddie slowly backed away. She would have given Tembah a run for his money, but the young black wolf seemed to have quickly calmed down and didn't try to antagonize Haddie.

As the afternoon drew near, Tembah joined the rest and napped. In a dream, he saw himself as the pack leader chasing prey. His legs and eyes twitched as he slept, engrossed in his dream. Tembah slept off and on all day. He woke up to see the pack getting restless for the night hunt. Tembah was now fully grown. He didn't like following the older wolves and began to run ahead of his siblings. Growler noticed but let it pass.

The night seemed to be fruitful and particularly useful for hunting. They worked together beautifully; however, the prey they encountered was just too fast. The rest of the night was uneventful until they encountered a dead bull moose. It lay on the ground, with most of the underside consumed by a bear. Growler stood momentarily, sniffed the air, and concluded it was safe to approach the moose. The pack moved onto the moose and ate plentifully. They kept watching for the bear that left the carcass behind as they ate. They ate their fill and then returned to the pack site with food for Breeze, the pups, and Maude.

The Rocky Hill pack lazily lay as the morning sun rose and summer approached. Tucker played happily with Haddie, then wrestled with Teebo for a while. Teebo finally rolled on his back as Tucker pretended to move in for the kill; his target, this time, was Tembah.

Tembah is a loaner; instead of playing with others, he'd find something else to do. Tucker should have known better because Tembah displayed his fangs and growled as he approached the big male. Tucker stood his ground, but Tembah jumped up and was on top of him before he knew it. It wasn't a long fight before Tucker started to run away.

Tembah caught up to him, and Tucker rolled on his back sub-missively. Tembah put his paw on Tucker's chest and then walked away. Teebo ran over to where Haddie was grooming herself and sat beside her.

As the summer gave way to fall, there were several occasions when Tembah had to be put in his place by one of the older wolves; he was becoming a problem. As time passed, it became apparent that Tembah was not a team player. Growler kept his eye on him. It would be a matter of time before the pack would get fed up with him, or like many young male wolves, Tembah would leave to form his own pack.

CHAPTER SIX

Joyce and Betty, Go To Lunch

The following day Joyce awoke to the sound of the back door slamming as Paul left for the day. He never liked to eat first thing in the morning, and she was thankful for that. Joyce knew she could finally relax only briefly because she had plenty to do. Leaving the comfort of her bed, she put on her housecoat and then made breakfast for Mike and herself

After breakfast, Mike asked his mom. "Can I let Sabean run and play with me in the yard after school?"

"As long as you make sure the gate is closed. You can play with Sabean as soon as you get home, but only for half an hour." Joyce explained.

"Just a half-hour, mom," Michael asked with annoyance in his voice."

"You don't want dad to catch you," Joyce said.

"Oh yeah, dad doesn't like anybody to be too happy and having fun," Michael said with a frown.

"Now, Michael, don't talk about your dad that way," Joyce said as she handed him his lunch and jacket.

Mike finished putting on his jacket and shoes and then tied up his laces. He stood up to find his mom standing in front of him. Joyce fussed with his collar, put her hands on his shoulders, closed her eyes, and prayed for her son's safety in Jesus' name."

"See you after school, Mike," Joyce said with a smile."

"Bye, mom," Michael shouted as he shut the door.

Joyce began to grind some coffee beans. The aroma filled her pretty, yellow kitchen, and she enjoyed the smell. Making her way to the bathroom, Joyce looked into the mirror; she began to repair her face and hair after a night of tossing and turning.

The phone rang, and she ran into the kitchen to answer it.

"Hello," Joyce said as she picked up the phone.

"Hi Joy, how are you doing?" Betty asked.

Betty Nolan is a thin, short lady with bright brown eyes. The two women had been friends for years and were more like sisters than just friends. They cared for each other very much. Even Michael thought of Betty as family and called her Aunt Betty.

"I'm okay," Joyce replied.

"I know that voice, Joy. Paul's been pushing you around again, hasn't he?" Betty said with concern in her voice.

"No, not really. Last night, he came home drunk. He didn't like what I made him for supper, so he threw it on the floor and went to bed," Joyce said.

"Come on, Joy; he's always picking on you for something. I don't know why you don't leave him?" Betty retorted.

"Paul told me if I tried to leave him, he'd hunt me down and kill me. I am too scared to take that chance," Joyce sighed, "I am so blessed to have you as a friend Betty."

"Well, you can't go on like this girl. How about I pick you up around noon, and we'll go for lunch." Betty invited.

"I don't have any money," Joyce replied.

"I'm buying, so I'll be there around noon," Betty said happily.

Getting out of the home and having lunch with her best friend inspired Joyce to dance around the kitchen gleefully. Her happiness turned to shame when she realized Betty always paid for everything. Paul only gives her enough money to get what they absolutely need to eat.

Betty's Smart car is red with a black top and a black streak running down the rear sides. She bought it and a motorcycle for her husband with the inheritance her father left her. She loved her little car. She put stuffed ladybugs on the dash and some stick-on ladybugs on her side windows. One of the best things is that it got around 60 km to a gallon and is very dependable. Her husband equipped it with cruise control and some other things, making it even more special to Betty.

Betty approached Joyce's place and turned in. She saw Sabean chained up and felt terrible for the animal. Betty got out of her car and started toward the wolfdog. Usually, Sabean would growl and bark loudly if someone came into the yard, but she knew Betty as a nice person and had met her before. Sabean's tail wagged as she approached her. Betty noticed how short the chain was and thought it had to be Paul that chained Sabean up like that; he seemed to be mean to everything. After rubbing the animal's head, she walked to Joyce's trailer and knocked on the door. Joy opened the door with her jacket already on.

"It looks like you're ready to go," Betty said, surprised.

"Just to get out for a bit is a privilege," Joyce said, smiling.

Betty offered to take her to the Big Bear Restaurant. Joy argued with her and said the Bently restaurant was good enough and cheaper."

"Oh, Betty, I feel so bad that I can't chip in, but Paul gives me only so much money every two weeks," Joy shared.

They got in the little smart car, which was amazingly spacious inside.

Betty started the car and commented, "He keeps you like a prisoner Joy just like he keeps that poor animal," Betty added, "You have never told me how you met him in the first place?"

Joyce's face softened, "I met him when I lived with my parents. He was so lovely to me, and for the first six months of marriage, he was everything I had hoped for in a husband, but then he met Brian Olsen and started to drink. He became a different man in a short time. It was like the drink had changed something in his head, and that's when he started pushing me around. Paul has never struck me, but he'll grab my hair or arm, which is painful." Joyce felt uncomfortable and changed the subject.

"You sure look nice, Betty," Joyce said as she looked at Betty up and down."

"Thanks, kid," Betty said with a smile.

Betty is very particular about what she wears and ensures that her coat, purse, and shoes match. Her coat was dark green, and she wore a lovely grey scarf with green stripes running through it. Her large purse was gray, as were her high heels.

"Paul said he is going away soon with Brian fishing or something, so I'll have the house to myself, and I can't wait," Joyce continued, "I guess I'm horrible for saying that, but I've found it hard to be around Paul. He seems so negative about most things, which brings me down too. I'm not sure why I still love him, but I do. I truly meant it when I said, in God's presence, 'for better or for worse.'

Joyce changed the conversation again, "I'm looking forward to the warmer weather; then I can at least go outside and work on my vegetable and flower gardens." Joyce declared.

Betty asked, "How do you manage? No matter what you are going through, you carry on. Your faith in God is admiral, but you must wonder why God let you marry Paul in the first place?" Betty queried.

Joyce looked sternly and said, "I wanted to marry Paul, so I can't blame God. I put myself in this situation. People are quick to blame God when, in fact, humans cause most of their own problems. Anyway, Jesus never leaves my side, and in knowing this, I'm never alone, which helps me. Friends and the Bible warned me about marrying a man like Paul because he is an unbeliever, but I didn't listen. I thought I could change him. God gave us free will because He didn't want robots. He wanted His people to be free to enjoy this world He created. The Bible warns us in 2 Corinthians 6:14,

Do not be unequally yoked together with unbelievers; for what fellowship has righteousness with lawlessness and what communion has light with darkness?

My feelings for Paul blinded me from God's warning. I didn't have peace but chalked it up to nerves." Joyce confessed.

Joy pointed out how humanity has caused horrific damage and destruction to the world. She said Matthew 24 tells us in the last days, people will be self-centered, and there will be increased crime and disrespect for authorities. I believe we're in the last days," Joyce continued, "The Bible calls what we are experiencing birth pangs before the onset of the Tribulation. God is waiting to make sure He leaves no one behind by giving everyone a chance to accept God's Son, but I wonder how long God will put up with everything."

Wow, you know your Bible, girl!" exclaimed Betty.

Joyce explained, "I have time after I clean the house, so I have gotten into God's word, and over time Jesus and I have formed a wonderful relationship. I cast all my cares on Him. When things get tough, I know Jesus, who knows suffering more than most, is with me and will get me through anything."

"I am so glad to hear you say this, and I must say I'm convicted. I know I better get into my Bible more and include Christ in my life," Betty confessed.

Joyce said, "Include Him in all aspects of your life, and you'll find a close relationship forming with the Savior like never before.

Betty and Joy drove around the little village of Bently. The village consisted of the Bently garage with gas, diesel, and a mechanic who could fix almost anything, the Janice Café, the Post Office, built at the turn of the century, as were most buildings there. On the other end of the block is

Laura's Boutique, which sells new and slightly used clothes, and a bulk food store. Across the road are a grocery store, the Bently Bank, a medical center, a pharmacy with a good selection of health needs, candy, batteries, etc., and a doctor who comes to town on Mondays, Wednesdays, and Fridays. Next to it is a bustling place, the Bently Bar & Liquor store. Finally stood another old building, Jack's Snacks & Stuff. As you leave the village, there are some new buildings, The Hungry Bear Restaurant and the Bently Restaurant.

Jack's Snacks & Stuff came into view. Betty asked Joy if she wasn't too hungry; perhaps they could browse around Jack's, which is always fun.

"I like the items he gets in," Betty announced, and Joyce nodded.

Jack's Snacks is a store that has a little of everything. Jack, the proprietor, is an old hippy who has owned the store since the seventies. He loves incense, and patchouli oil is his favorite. Upon entering, Betty said she'd be right back. She went through a heavy steel door that led to a room with food items to see if there were any muffins. The smell of incense couldn't get through that thick door. Joyce wandered around the store and noticed a counter full of camouflage baseball caps and jackets; all his products for sale smelled like patchouli oil. It is almost an advertising ploy because if the locals smelled Patchouli oil on a person, they knew they had been at Jack's, indicating the store might have new things to sell. It was always interesting to shop at Jack's Snacks.

Betty joined her and said, "No muffins today. Old Jack still hasn't sold all the camouflage clothing yet, and the cost has dropped even more."

Joyce said, "I know Michael would love a new ball cap. He looks forward to watching a weekly TV show with some Christian guys down south that wear camouflaged clothes, so he'd be over the moon with this cap.

"Get one for him," Betty urged.

"Even at $5 a cap, I can't afford one. Joyce answered.

"I'll get one for the little dude, and don't try to talk me out of it," Betty said, placing her finger over Joyce's mouth.

"Thank you, Betty, he'll love it," Joy replied.

Betty noticed men's jackets as they were leaving, but they were all too big for Michael. They returned to the car.

The Hungry Bear Restaurant was less than a km away. They found a parking spot near the front door. The restaurant's decor was rustic, with pictures of the old days in Bently and the area.

The waitress showed them to a booth and laid down two menus.

"Everything looks so good but expensive," Joyce said.

"Don't worry about it. I just got paid, and my overtime was on my check, so pick anything you like, my friend. I'm going to have a steak sandwich," Betty said, smiling.

"Oh, Betty, it's been a long time since I had a steak. Would it be okay with you if I had a steak sandwich too?" Joy requested.

"If that's what you want, go for it," Betty said as she patted Joyce's hand, "I hope you know I am always here for you, pal?" Betty whispered.

"I know, and I thank God you are. I'm so blessed that you allow me to vent my feelings and get me out of my place," Joyce looked down.

The waitress brought over their lunches. They both relished every mouthful. The two women enjoyed each other's company for most of the afternoon. Full and satisfied, Betty got up and paid the bill, then they left.

Joyce said, "Betty, thank you for lunch and this time out, but I'd better head home. Mike will be home from school soon."

They drove into Joy's driveway just as Michael's smiling face entered the yard.

"Hi, mom. I've shut the gate, so I'll let Sabean off her chain to play with me." Mike yelled.

"Okay!" his mom answered, "but you might want to see what Aunt Betty bought you first."

"For me, how come?" Mike asked, with his face beaming as he looked at Betty.

"You know me, Mike, I just love to see you smile," Betty replied, handing him the bag. The boy pulled out the cap and shrieked with glee.

"Wow, it's just like what the guys wear on TV. Thank you so much, Aunty Betty. I love it,"

Mike said as he removed his old cap and put the new one on. He hugged Betty, handed his old cap to Joyce, then turned and said to Sabean, "Look what I got, girl."

He ran over to the wolfdog. Sabean sniffed at Mike's cap and was curious about its smell, then rubbed her face on the grass.

Joyce said sheepishly, "Thanks again, Betty, but I'd better get supper started if Paul comes home on time."

"Okay, Joyce, it's getting a bit late, so I'll be on my way," Betty announced.

They hugged each other and said goodbye. Joyce went inside her home. Michael took the hook off Sabine's neck chain and ran around the yard with the animal close behind him. Grabbing a ball, he turned around and yelled, "Go get it, girl."

Sabean ran after the ball, grabbed it, then ran away. Mike laughed and started to chase her. Sabean would stop just long enough for the boy to catch up, and then she'd race away again.

Joyce looked out the kitchen window, and a big grin appeared. It was so lovely to see her son and Sabean having fun. She took some ground beef from the fridge and began to make meatballs and spaghetti.

Mike called Sabean to stop running. Tired and winded from play, Michael stopped and beckoned Sabean to come. The wolfdog started running toward him fast and knocked the boy off his feet onto the wet ground. She began licking Mike's face as the boy laughed and tried to get up. In the process of standing, his new cap fell to the ground. Sabean grabbed it and ran around the yard with Mike following, then the animal stopped. Mike grabbed the cap and said, "Let go of my cap, girl."

Sabean obeyed, gave the cap back without a fight, and licked his face as Mike tried to put it back on. Finally, Michael led Sabean to her stake and hooked the collar back on but hooked the end of her collar further down the chain to give her more room.

He kneeled, hugged the animal, and said, "I love you, Sabean."

Mike headed for the trailer, entered, and told his mom about the fun he had just experienced with Sabean.

Mike was still talking when he heard his father's truck drive in. Paul slammed the door of the truck.

"I'll be in my room, mom, Michael said.

Paul unlocked the door. He removed his jacket and dropped it on the floor as he went to the living room. He slumped down into his big, padded chair, placed his shoes on the footstool, and yelled, "Joyce, get me a beer!"

Joyce stopped stirring the meat sauce. She opened the fridge and realized that there was more beer than food.

"What's taking you so long?" Paul shouted.

Sitting the beer on the counter, she opened it, then hurried into the living room and said,

"How was your day?"

"Bad as usual, but I guess you had a day of leisure watching your soaps." snarled Paul.

Joyce thought to herself; except for going out with Betty, which is seldom, she didn't usually have time to sit around all day watching soaps. Paul's comment bothered her.

"I hardly sat around watching TV all day, Paul," Joyce said.

"Oh, come on, you can't call a bit of housework and cooking real work," Paul said sarcastically.

Joyce knew better than to argue with him and retreated to the kitchen again to finish the spaghetti sauce. She put the pasta in a boiling pot on the stove. Michael exited his room and asked, "Hi, mom, whatcha doing?"

"Getting dinner ready, dear, now keep quiet; remember, dad is home," she replied.

Michael knew what she meant, and his happy body language changed to sadness.

Joyce put the stove on low and then began to set the table. As she placed the dishes on the table, she wondered how dinner would go. Would Paul pick on her, or is it Michael's turn to be hassled? She prayed that Paul would go out after dinner or watch a game on TV, keeping him entertained so they would be out of the line of fire. Joyce could hear Paul phoning someone.

"Hey, Brian, want to grab a six-pack and come over for the game tonight?" Paul asked, then continued, "Okay, see you after dinner."

Joyce was relieved that Paul would be busy with Brian but knew they would be loud once they had a few beers under their belts. She started to think about what kind of snacks they would expect. There wasn't enough money left from her grocery money to buy chips or nuts, but she did have flour; she would have to bake something right after dinner. Joyce placed the dinner on the table.

"Paul, supper is ready," she called.

"Wait a minute!" Paul yelled angrily.

Paul put the TV on and started watching the pre-game show. She realized he wanted dinner in the living room and brought him a TV table. Glued to the TV, Paul finally got up, walked to the kitchen, filled his plate, and returned to his chair.

Michael smiled at his mom and sat down for dinner. The young boy began to relax at the table with his mom. They had a nice quiet dinner without Paul—no comments accusing Mike of eating like a pig or something else. Eating supper with his dad is a stressful experience. Mike was glad to sit and eat without constantly looking up to see if he somehow displeased his father.

Brian knocked on the door. Joyce opened it. Without acknowledging her, he walked in. Brian had a low opinion of women.

"Hurry up; the game has already started," Paul beckoned.

Brian sat on the couch, and Joyce brought him a beer without being asked.

"Thanks," Brian said, staring at the TV.

Brian is a short heavyset man. He could be friendly if he wanted to be.

The rest of the night went okay. Joy made some cookies and put them on the coffee table without a thank you. Joyce became tired and said she was going to bed.

Paul grunted a response, then yelled as his team made a good play.

CHAPTER SEVEN

Alfred's First Visit To His Granddad's

Al woke up and lay in his bed thinking about his grandfather. Bert and his family were away for a week, so Al decided to visit his granddad.

Today was the last day of school before the summer holidays. Alfred had never been too excited about holidays unless Bert was around; otherwise, he would sit outside, daydream, or sleep. Sleep was often Alfie's escape from life.

Alf got out of bed, dressed, and filled his pillowcase with PJs, underwear, and a toothbrush; he put it under his pillow, then went down the stairs, grabbed a piece of pizza, and opened the back door. He felt great freedom, knowing he would soon be with someone who cared about him.

Alfred would have to walk a long way to reach his grandfather's cabin. Al thought if he power-walked, he might reach the cabin by eight or nine pm. He planned to stay with him for a week.

Bert was waiting for Alfred outside with a massive grin on his face.

"Guess what? I passed my driver's license!" Bert said with pride.

"Wow, you can go anywhere you want now," Al said.

"Well, not entirely, because my dad will decide when I'm ready to drive independently. Dad is very protective of me, Alf. I must admit that I feel safe when dad is with me until I get comfortable driving. I think I told you we leave tonight for my grandma's place for a few days, and dad said I could drive us there and back," replied Bert.

"That tells you something, Bert. Your mom and dad must feel safe with you behind the wheel," Al encouraged.

Al stopped Bert, took him aside, and shared in a low voice, "I'm going to see my grandfather while you are gone, and I'm not going to tell my family."

"I won't tell them, but what if your mom and dad get worried," Bert whispered.

"Bert, they won't be the least bit worried. I doubt they will even know I'm gone," Al shared.

"I'm going to power-walk as I taught you, so it shouldn't take long; you're still practicing it, aren't you?" asked Alf.

"I sure am and can prove it; let's power-walk the rest of the way to school," Bert suggested, and off they went.

It was the last day of school, and the kids would receive their report cards. Al knew he had probably failed. He thought to himself, what a way to start the summer holidays. The school day dragged on. Just before their early release, he got his report card; he was right; he failed miserably, except for an excellent math mark.

The bell rang, and the summer holidays had finally materialized. Alfred walked slowly out of the school's exit doors and the few blocks home. When he entered the house, he found his mother on the couch, awake but drunk. Al handed her the report card. Darlene screamed at him and told him to get out of her sight. Al gladly obliged, ran upstairs, grabbed the pillowcase under his pillow, ran downstairs, and left the house without looking at his mom.

Alfred loved sports, and one day he saw men in a power-walking contest. Al started practicing every day and became quite accomplished.

He approached the ten km mark out of town, still full of energy. Al has strong legs and excellent lungs, making him a natural power-walker. Alfred can power-walk for miles without breathing heavily. It didn't take long before he reached Phyllis Falls. He sat down to rest for a short time and enjoyed the lake's breathtaking view and the falls. A couple of geese and their young had made their summer home near the lake's left side. This lake's beauty draws visitors annually. There are a few amenities for the visitors and nearby campers; a laundromat, a general store, a gas station, and a place to buy burgers, hot dogs, pop, and soft ice cream. Many picnic tables are also available near the lake. In the vicinity are two campgrounds, one about a km east and the other about twenty km away. The campers depend on Phyllis Falls for their needs. Captivated by the lake scenery, Alfred rested longer than he intended, but finally, he returned to reality and focused on his journey.

Alfred was on a mission. He got up and started power-walking with determination the rest of the way. It was getting dark when Al reached a sign cautioning people to beware of wildlife. Alfie looked over the map he got from his grand-father. It was a little unclear which path to take to get to the cabin. He decided to take the path just past the warning sign. The weedy, overgrown path with prickly bushes seemed to reach out to grab and scratch him on purpose. Small annual trees with long thin branches latched onto his shirt like eagle talons; one taller bush branch managed to rip off his cap. He received more scratches as he retrieved it. Soon after, the path opened up to a large area. Al could see smoke coming from a cabin chimney, and he felt relieved to know he was almost there when the thought hit him; what if this isn't granddad's place? He walked across to the cabin. The map was easy to follow except for the path. Al thought he wouldn't have found this place without the map. He was convinced he followed the map right, but he looked it over again to make sure. Al proceeded to the door and knocked; he could hear someone rustling inside.

"Who's there?" Bill asked as he looked through a peek hole in the door. The door opened, and Alfred opened his arms wide.

He said, "Hi, granddad."

Bill smiled and embraced him. They hugged each other for quite a while.

"What are you doing out here at this time of night? Come in, boy, and sit down." Bill said,

"You have no idea how much I've missed you. I prayed for you to come, and here you are, praise God."

Alf said, "I missed you and just had to see you. I left as soon as school was out. I power-walked all the way here."

"Power-walked? How do you do that? Bill questioned.

"I'll show you tomorrow," Al promised, then asked how Bill felt about having him stay for a week.

"A week, praise the Lord, that's good by me. Stay as long as you like, anytime." Bill said joyfully.

Alfred could feel the weight of his problems disappear. He sat listening to the old man as he put more wood in the potbelly stove in the middle of the cabin.

The cabin was humble, as was Bill himself. It had a peaceful feeling about it. For the first time in a long time, Alfred felt at peace.

When Bill talked to him, Al absorbed and retained every word he heard. There was something about his granddad that was uniquely different from most folks. Bill fascinated him. Alfie asked him how he could live such a worry-free life and survive even when food was hard to get at times. With a broad smile that showed his few teeth left, Bill simply said, "Jesus!"

Bill Dennis loved his daughter's unwanted son, Alfred. He found great joy in teaching him many things, especially about his relationship with God. Bill's patience paid off because it enabled him to teach Alfred, and the young fellow responded and learned quickly. He never stuttered or felt nervous around his grandfather as he did at home. Alfred needed encouragement, someone to show him the way through his troubled life, and Bill was that someone.

It was nearly midnight, so Bill announced it was time for bed. Al stood up, and as he did, Bill handed him a big bag.

"What's this?" Alfred wondered out loud.

"Open it up," Bill prompted.

Alfred's happy face shone as he pulled out the camouflage cap and jacket. He tried them on, and they fit nicely. Bill explained that he bought the same jacket and cap at Jack's Snacks and thought of him. Alfred felt special and couldn't help but hug his grandfather again. He hung up the jacket and put the cap on the hook; he turned to Bill and smiled,

"Thank you for buying those things for me. May I keep them here because mom doesn't like people giving me things?" Al asked. Bill said he understood and that the jacket and cap would be waiting for him.

Bill asserted, "Before hitting the hay, I suggest you use the outhouse. You'll find it behind the cabin about fifty paces south. I have some fluorescent-painted sticks that help show the way. Make lots of noise, so the animals hear you and leave." Bill handed the boy a flashlight.

Alfred didn't want to admit it, but he was scared. He went outside to the back of the cabin, and all he could see at first was blackness. After a moment, his eyes adjusted, and he could see the fluorescent-painted sticks. The flashlight the old man gave him was one of those small ones. It gave off just enough light to see a bit before him, but soon, the outhouse appeared. While Al was inside, he heard wild animal sounds that frightened him. He hurried, opened the door, and quickly moved back to the safety of the cabin.

"Find the outhouse, boy?" Bill asked.

"No problem," responded Al.

"Great, I was worried you might not find it and get lost," old Bill said.

"Not me. I have good eyes in the dark, and I wasn't afraid." Al lied.

He didn't fool Bill a bit, and he smiled to himself as he got into bed. He thought Alfred was so much like him when he was young. Bill used to be prideful and independent; he didn't want to show weakness.

As Bill lay in bed, he told Alfred, "Before you fall asleep, think about your day, thank God in Jesus' name for guiding you through it, and confess any sins and ask for forgiveness.

"I will," Alfred replied.

Bill's armless brown couch made an excellent bed for Alfred. Bill had pulled out a sleeping bag and pillow from under the couch. He had them in a bag to keep them clean. He gave them to Alfred. Al let out a loud sleepy sigh and said goodnight. Bill said goodnight and turned out the kerosene lamp.

The morning sun shone through the window beside the door; the warmth of it made Alf smile with contentment. Bill brought wood in and threw some inside the stove. It wasn't long before Alf could smell coffee getting stronger; he rubbed his eyes.

"So, you're awake, boy," Bill said with a twinkle in his eyes, then added, "I'm making some pancakes." Alfred grinned widely.

Bill asked how many Alf would like, and the boy answered one hundred and laughed.

"You'll have to teach me how to cook. I don't even know how to cook. I'm just stupid," Al confessed.

Bill answered him with a grin, "Hang around me. You're a quick learner. You must overcome putting yourself down because you are far from stupid."

After breakfast, the two went to check Bill's traps. They were empty. They walked over to the campground, and Bill showed Al around. Al gave Bill a demonstration on how to power-walk. Bill was impressed but said he'd prefer to walk normally. They walked around the various sites and came to a deep ravine with a warning sign. It warned people not to step too close to the ravine's edge because the earth was unstable. Alfred couldn't help himself. He walked past the warning sign and looked down. Al let out a low whistle because it was a long way down.

Bill became upset and bellowed, "What are you doing? You could fall off. Please come here right now!"

Realizing his foolishness, Alfred approached Bill and said he was sorry.

The old chap told him how much Al meant to him, but he had to follow the rules. Al said he would in the future. They walked back to the cabin.

Bill said, "Let's have a game of checkers before lunch," Bill invited.

"Okay," replied Al.

The old boy won all three games, then announced, "Getting hungry?"

"Starving," the young man answered eagerly.

The old guy went to the window, kneeled, and removed the floor mat and a floorboard, uncovering the fair-sized hole. Bill disappeared down the hole. He grabbed a pot of stew from one of the shelves in his cellar. Alfred wondered what his grandfather was doing. Hands finally appeared, holding a pot; putting the pot down beside the hole on the floor, Bill climbed back up.

"How do you like my fridge?" Bill said as he emerged. His arthritis made him groan a bit as he stood up. Bill picked up the stew pot and put it on the stove. He then replaced the floorboard and mat that covered the hole. No one would ever guess there was a cellar under the cabin.

"How much room do you have down there?" asked Alf.

"Go and check it out," Bill prompted.

"Okay," Alf said, removing the mat and floorboard. Alfred stepped down carefully, and Bill handed him the flashlight. Alfred was impressed with the cellar, and with his curiosity satisfied, Al climbed back up.

Alf told Bill, "You never cease to amaze me."

The old stove heated the pot, and it wasn't long before the smell of stew filled the one-room cabin. Bill grabbed a couple of bowls, filled them, and placed them on the small wooden table at the end of Bill's bed.

"You sure make great stew," Alfred commented as he finished the last spoonful in his bowl.

"Thanks, boy. Not too much to it, just wild herbs, garlic, and rabbit meat," Bill replied.

"I wish I knew all the stuff you know," the young man said.

Bill looked fondly at the young man and said, "You will. Do you know you're my favorite grandson? I want you to have the land and cabin when I die. I have put those instructions in my Will, but don't tell Larry or your folks, okay?"

"I won't tell them." Alfred agreed and said, "Wow, you will," pausing to digest the announcement, "but I don't want you to die." the young guy said with sadness on his face."

"I don't intend to leave this earth just yet," Bill confided.

Alfred said, "I hope you live a long time," Alfie paused, then added, "I hope you love me as much as you say because you will have to get used to me being around all the time. Mom said she'll kick me out if I fail school next year."

Bill commented, "That sounds like your mother; I guess that means you failed this year. If you fail next year, you have a home with me."

"I'll teach you everything I know, and I am sure you'll catch on to things fast. Alfred, you're not stupid," Bill assured him.

Alfred shook his head sadly and said, "I think I am."

"What do you mean?" Bill's forehead wrinkled.

Alfie lowered his head and confessed, "Mom, Dad, Larry, and everyone else says so. I can't seem to concentrate on what's going on at school either. The school counselor said I was borderline retarded, and only capable of labor jobs when I leave school."

"They are wrong," declared Bill. You're not interested enough to keep that kind of stuff in your head. You're a sharp kid, and it won't take long before living on the land will become second nature to you. Your brother could never learn what I will teach you, but you have to come out here more often. I'm darn proud of you. Everything I teach you sticks in that brain of yours," he assured him.

"Wow, I guess it does," thought Al.

"It's hard for me to believe you actually want me and not think of me as stupid," Al confessed.

The old man beamed, "My home is your home. Feel free to move in anytime after you finish school next year.

"Yes! That will be great!" exclaimed Alfred as he jumped forward and hugged Bill, almost knocking the old fellow over in the process.

Al had wanted to be with his grandfather since he was eight when Bill first started visiting his family.

Bill added, "You will never lose the land. This land has been in our family for more than ninety-five years. It lies right on the border of Jersey and Richmond Counties. That's why they could put that public campground close to my place because it rests on Jersey County land, and the rules are different there."

The young man thought that once the cabin was his home, life would be worth living, and he'd have a purpose. He could do all the hard work and let his beloved grandfather live more comfortably. With Bill's influence, wisdom, and encouragement, Alf thought he could be as bright as the next guy. For the first time in Alfred's life, he had a future. Al was going to look after his granddad while learning everything he could from him.

"Thanks be to God! You're a strong young guy, and I'm sure you'll greatly help me. I love you, Alfred," Bill said excitedly.

Al smiled, "Thank you so much."

"Come on, let's wash up the dishes, then go for a walk," Bill suggested.

Bill shared his salvation story with Alfie as they wandered on the property.

"I was nursing a coffee at the Charlie Bean Coffee Cafe in Whitewolf. A Pastor named Dale Scott was passing through town and stopped at the coffee café. It was busy, but he saw me sitting by myself and asked if he could join me. We introduced ourselves and talked a bit, then ordered more coffee. Dale asked me if I knew Jesus. He explained things about God I never knew." Bill said.

I asked him, "Can you explain why some so-called Christians look down on people like me, and what about all the wars fought over religion?

Dale said, "Not all people who claim to be Christians are. In fact, many seekers of Christ get turned off because of a few people who think of themselves as better than others. Jesus seekers must focus on Jesus and not on the people. The Bible says in Matthew 13:24-30

Jesus told them another parable: "The kingdom of heaven is like a man who sowed good seed in his field. But while everyone was sleeping, his enemy came and sowed weeds among the wheat and went away. When the wheat sprouted and formed heads, then the weeds also appeared. "The owner's servants came to him and said, `Sir, didn't you sow good seed in your field? Where then did the weeds come from?' "`An enemy did this,' he replied. "The servants asked him, `Do you want us to go and pull them up?' "`No,' he answered, `because while you are pulling the weeds, you may root up the wheat with them. Let both grow together until the harvest. At that time, I will tell the harvesters: First, collect the weeds and tie them in bundles to be burned; then gather the wheat and bring it into my barn.'"

"In other words, in most churches, you will find good and not-so-good people. Just because they attend church doesn't mean they live for Christ or they wouldn't act that way toward others. That kind of attitude has deterred many people from seeking the Lord altogether.

I expressed how it must sadden Jesus when people give up on Him because of how some people treated them.

Dale added, "They forget people are not Christ and, therefore, imperfect like Him. Some lose the opportunity to have a relationship and a better life with Jesus just because they don't feel accepted by people, and often blame God for their loss of interest."

"I don't understand why Jesus is the only way to God. What about all those holy type people who practice Hinduism, Buddha, Confucianism, etc.," Bill asked.

Dale asked, "Did any of them take our sins upon themselves like Jesus and pay for them by sacrificing themselves to God? He willingly paid the price for our sins on the cross to restore humanity's relationship with God. Are any of those other religions' founders, teachers, or prophets alive?"

"I don't think so," Bill confessed.

Dale continued, "Right, Jesus, the son of God, is still living. After Christ died on the cross, He rose from the dead alive on the third day. Jesus appeared to His disciples and over 500 people in the forty days before ascending back to Heaven. Through our living Jesus, He will raise us up one day, sanctified by Christ's sacrifice, never to perish, and live in the kingdom of God forever. Dale quoted John 14:6a.

John 14:6

Jesus answered, "I am the way and the truth and the life. No one comes to the Father except through me."

"You see, my friend, Jesus is alive, and it's through Him and only Him can we approach God," Dale explained,

"Before Christ came, people would sacrifice perfect animals without flaws to remove sin from them. They had to do that often because they continued to sin. Jesus is the perfect sacrifice, and He gave Himself to pay painfully on the cross for our sins. No more sacrifices are necessary. If you repent and confess your sins, Jesus will forgive you.

"I've read a bit of the Bible. It says that whatever you want, ask God in the name of Jesus, and you will receive it. I tried that a few times, and nothing happened," Bill remarked.

God has a plan for our lives, so if you ask for something that fits His plan, you will receive it. However, He won't grant your request if your request is not to your benefit. It may be that timing is wrong because he knows what's ahead, or He has something better for you."

"Now I'm starting to understand," Bill stated as he ordered more coffee.

Dale said, "God gave man free will, but what man does with that freedom of choice is up to him. Some people who go to churches don't always choose God's will. Remember, not all churches are like the one you went to. God might have drawn you to that church to see the difference between a non-committed Christian and the walking-talking Christian," explained Dale.

"I told the Pastor about my granny, Willamina, or Mini, as her friends called her. She told me about Jesus when I was around six. I think she planted a seed of God in me." Bill shared, "Granny left her Bible to me when she died, so I started to read it. I surmised that If I followed God's Commandments, I could change into a good man. I thought

I had found the answer, but the more I tried to follow the Commandments, the more I sinned. God knew I was seeking Him, and I think He sent you, Pastor Dale, to help me," confessed Bill.

Dale took out his Bible. He told me he usually reads from the New King James Bible but sometimes finds it challenging for some new believers to understand. In contrast, the Living Bible or the Message Bible is easier to understand. I often check both Bibles to ensure I get the point of what I am reading," Some verses are so long that I can see it might confuse some. As an example, Paul wrote Romans 7:14-25. It tells us why we need Jesus to help us on the right path. It explains that the Law of God is good, righteous, and holy. It helps us see how sinful our sin nature really is. Without the Law, we would convince ourselves that our sin was not that bad, especially when we compared our sin to others. However, we learn from the Bible that all of us are judged equally by the Law of God, and none of us can keep it. That is why we need Jesus.

"So, you see, Bill, we need Jesus to straighten out our lives. We can't do it alone. It doesn't mean we should intentionally sin, but once He convicts us of sin, we should ask Jesus to forgive us, and He will. God knows we can't help being sinners, so that's why God sent his only son to earth to show us the way of righteousness and pay the ultimate sacrifice for our sins. The last thing Jesus said before He died was, "It is finished,"

Bill thought about what the Pastor was saying and then asked if God created everything, why did He create evil?

Dale replied, "God didn't create evil, but He does allow it. Adam and Eve believed Satan in The Garden of Eden and allowed evil to enter them. God allows evil because He gave us free will, and we can choose whether or not we want to serve the Lord or ourselves. If God didn't allow evil to happen, we would have no choice and serve God out of obligation, not by choice.

Bill said, "Those verses helped me understand God better. The Pastor also pointed out how important it was to read God's word and get to know Him. God speaks to us through the scriptures. Dale showed me how praying to Jesus and walking in His way can change a person into someone who will put Jesus first in their life.

"God has blessed me repeatedly since then, Alfred." Bill said, "I do what I can to help others and hope I get an opportunity to share Jesus. I pray to Jesus to have His way in my life and help me face my problems. He may not remove the problems but will walk me through them. I love Jesus for what He did on the cross for all of us, including you, Alfie.

I had more questions, so Dale offered to stay a few days. I was happy that he cared enough to stay. The pastor taught me to embrace life as an obedient Christian. He promised Jesus would never turn His back on me. God tells us that in this world, we will have tribulations. He knows the challenges life will give us. God allows even evil things to teach us how to approach problems by depending on Him. For instance, when we decide to do something without asking for God's guidance, we're on our own and often fail. We wonder why the things we sometimes try turn out wrong. I don't do anything now without praying for God's will and guidance before starting something. He'll give us peace if it corresponds to His plan for us. If I don't have peace about what I want to do, I put it aside and leave it with God," The old man relayed.

Dale picked up his Bible and turned to Proverbs. 3:5-6

Trust in the Lord with all your heart, and
do not rely on your own insight.

In all your ways, acknowledge him, and
he will make straight your paths.'

"The pastor taught me to walk in God's will and love Jesus and his message. According to God's word, He helps us. I also had to learn to love myself in a balanced way and forgive my weaknesses. I was once a very proud man and didn't like to depend on anyone else. If I asked for help, I felt I would be beholding to that person. I'd get mad when I failed at something and often called myself stupid. Learning to love myself was hard for me initially. I was overwhelmed with joy to learn that God loved and accepted me just as I was, but He saw my potential and wanted to bring that out in me over time," Bill concluded.

"God's timing is perfect. God knows when you're ready for each change, He makes. You know, Bill, God knows more about us than we do. After all, He made us," Dale pointed out.

Bill told Alfred, "I invited Christ into my heart and life that day, and such a peace flooded my whole being."

"Pastor Scott had to leave, and I never saw him again, but I hold Dale dear in my heart and pray that God will protect him as He uses him to bring people to Christ. " Bill said.

Alfred understood Jesus better and fully accepted Him as his Savior that afternoon, making Bill ecstatic for his grandson.

"Grandfather, I have a friend. His name is Bert Black. We go to school and hang out together. Bert has a loving family, and they are good to me. I am unsure if I could have made it this long in life if I didn't have Bert, especially after you stopped visiting. I knew you stopped because my mom and family didn't respect you. Mom's drinking made you sad. I understood you didn't want to see her that way. By the way, would you mind if I brought Bert here to meet you someday?" Alfred queried.

"That would be fine." Bill agreed.

Do you ever get lonely?" asked Alfie.

He rubbed his face and looked thoughtful, then related, "I do get a little lonely sometimes, but the fact is Jesus said he will never leave me, so I know I'm not alone. If I see someone needing help, I am glad to help them, as the Lord told us to do. After I help them with their need, I tell them about the good news of Jesus Christ. Some want to hear more and agree, or they decide to disagree. What people do with the knowledge of Christ is up to them and God, who loves them. I have to admit I've always been a loaner. The Holy Spirit is working on changing that in me."

"I know what you mean," the young man agreed.

Bill said he loved where he lived. He pointed out it was usually pretty quiet; however, in the summer months, I can hear people at the campground when they turned up their music, which drowned out God's nature song. Fortunately, the campers usually leave on Sunday to return to work," Bill smiled, then added, "I must admit I like some of the music they play."

"Do you ever get bears near the cabin?" Alfie asked.

Bill thought for a while, then answered, "There were a couple of times over the years, but all the animals know me now, and I belong here. They don't seem to bother me, nor do I bother them."

Bill has a healthy respect for meat-eating animals. He knows most of the territories they call home and keeps to his land.

"I hope you'll like it out here, son. There is so much to do. The only fun is trying to beat this old man at checkers or cards. Think about it, Al, no gyms where you can work out or fun places to go, but if nothing else, you'll get in shape. It's a good plan. It tells us in Matthew 18:20,

For where two gather in my name, there am I with them, so let us pray to Jesus to guide you regarding moving in with me and see if it is in God's plan.

After praying, Bill stood up from his chair and began to clean up when Alfred took over and said, smiling, "I might as well start earning my place around here."

Bill encouraged, "Help yourself, and thank you, Alfred."

After a while, Bill put his sweater on and said, "Time to check the traps, so let's get going.

After an extensive walk on the land, they had one fat squirrel. Bill deposited the squirrel into a sack and said, "Squirrel soup," with a grin.

He suggested they walk back to the cabin via the campground. The place seemed empty except for a small tent occupied by someone who could snore louder than they had ever heard. Al saw the warning sign by the ravine's edge and stayed clear.

Bill said, "I don't need to go far to find something to eat out here."

"Yeah, I guess there are many rabbits and squirrels," Alf said.

Bill answered, "There are more than just animals to eat, Al. The good Lord is a good provider. Bill adjusted his cap and said, "People don't know what they're missing without Jesus in their lives."

The young man looked up and told Bill that it was too bad that some people don't respect God as they should, and it must sadden Jesus when people don't want Him in their lives.

Bill shared an old story he had heard. "A couple invited God to their home. God came into their house and sat down; they gave him a cup of coffee and said they would return soon to visit, but they got busy with life and forgot Him. God waited at the table alone all day; finally, He got up and left.

Alfred shook his head sadly as they slowly walked back to the cabin. Bill sighed and stated,

"Many people just don't make time for God and wonder why they don't have a closer relationship with Him. In the book of Revelation, the Bible talks about various churches; the last church is called the Laodicea church. That church talks about how people are in the last days regarding God; they are neither hot nor cold but only lukewarm toward our

Maker. We need to give our all to Jesus and put Him first in our lives, and He will help us along our life's path."

They entered the cabin, and Alfie sat down. Bill stood by the window and looked far into the woods.

Bill commented, "Jesus is very patient and will allow everyone to see how much they need Him and how much He loves them. In some trials, God teaches us how to handle problems we face now and in the future. He wants to help people with everything in their lives; all they have to do is ask."

Alfred looked at Bill, and with a big grin, he yelled, "I can't wait to come and live with you!"

"I can't wait either! I'm getting old and could use an extra pair of hands." Bill admitted.

"Except for math class, I'm not really interested in school. I can't seem to get serious about the other subjects and end up daydreaming. When it comes to tests, I forget even the stuff I learned. My mind goes blank," Alfie confided.

"I think you have a heart for nature more than an academic heart," Bill said as he looked Al in the eyes.

The day was almost over, and darkness began to move in. The country has no lights, so the nighttime is pitch black.

"Let's get our jackets on and sit around the fire pit outside," Bill invited.

The two sat on a big fireside bench Bill had made. The old fellow grabbed some wood there and started a fire. The fire soon took hold while Bill and Al stared at it as it crackled and sparked.

After a while, Bill asked, "Are you getting too warm?"

"Yes, I am," Al replied.

The old guy's face filled with excitement, "Now, my boy, stand up and turn around and see the Glory of God." Bill said as Al stood and turned. Bill quoted the Bible as he pointed to the star-filled sky. Alfred gazed in wonderment, and he exclaimed, "Wow!"

Psalms 8:3-4

3. When I consider Your heavens, the work of your fingers, the moon, and the stars, which you have set in place, 4. what is mankind that you are mindful of them, human beings that you care for them?

The sky was filled with seemingly billions of stars, accentuating the black night. After a while, their backs started to get too warm.

Bill said, "Ready to turn back around?"

Alfred nodded; they turned back toward the fire and sat back down.

"You know Proverbs 23:7 that I taught you, Alfred. You are what you think you are. It's all about building your confidence and not giving up on yourself."

Bill stood up and stretched, then sat back down and commented, "We all have two sides inside our hearts. One side can be evil and full of anger, envy, greed, arrogance, self-pity, guilt, and so on. Do you think and feel some of that in your life? Bill asked.

"I wish I didn't, but I must admit, the bad side is in me," Al answered shamefully.

"Ah, but the other side is good, peaceful, loving, hopeful, humble, kind, benevolent, compassionate, etc. Do you have any of these traits?" Bill inquired.

"I think I have some of those traits but not all. How does knowing this help my confidence?"Alfie coaxed.

"We must intentionally try to bring out our good side every chance we get. That way, thinking and exhibiting those good thoughts make us confident in our actions and happier in life. It takes a lot of practice to control our feelings and thoughts, but it is worth the effort." Bill encouraged.

Bill moved the embers around, and as he did, Alfie looked up at the sky and watched the sparks embrace the blackness. Some large bushes began to move wildly about as an animal passed through them. Alfred's eyes grew big.

The old man smiled and said, "Whatever is moving through the bush, better be quiet, or it will end up as Mr. bear's dinner." They both laughed.

"I guess it can be exciting living out here," Alfred questioned as he looked into the darkness surrounding them.

His grandfather said, "I love it out here, although I must admit that sometimes loneliness enters my heart, especially in the winter when no one is around."

Al thought about that and felt bad for the old man. Bill stood up and stretched.

"I look forward to sharing my life with you, my boy; I'll never be lonely again," Bill confirmed, "Tomorrow, we'll be rechecking the campground; I check daily and try to keep a close eye on things there," He paused, then added, "After all, the owner depends on me to keep watch on the place and take the money from the campers. He pays me more than he should. I think I have a pretty good deal. I have sharp hearing, and I know when people are there. I've met some friendly folks there too. I met a lady, Joyce was her name, a few weeks ago, and we had a lovely talk. She served me a cup of iced tea, then we sat down and had a wonderful conversation about the Lord until her husband started rowing to shore. Joyce said she'd better get her husband's lunch. I thanked her for the drink and conversation. As I turned to leave, I waved at her husband, but he didn't return the gesture, then I left." Bill concluded.

"I know I'll probably fail next year too. I can look for another place to live if you feel I might be a bother to have around all the time," Alfie confessed.

"You won't be a bother; you'll be a help to me around here," Bill stated.

Alfred loved hearing he was needed and would have a purpose in life. Changing the subject

Alfie asked. "Tell me, what was it like growing up here?

Bill thought for a moment, then replied, "When I was a young boy, the animals scared me a bit, but they have never bothered me, and I don't bother them. I only trap small critters.

"You're starting to look tired, kid, so let's go inside. Tomorrow, I'll teach you more things if you're up for it," Bill said as he stood up.

The following day the sun was bright, and the air was full of bird songs.

"Come on, Alfred. The day awaits us." Bill enticed.

After breakfast, they strolled around the property. They spent the day talking, picking herbs, checking traps, and the campground until the sun started to go down.

Bill headed for the fire pit and started a fire with a few sticks. Alfred gathered some wood and carefully added them; they sat silently for some time, enjoying the fire.

The fire was going out, and as Bill reached for more wood, he noticed Alfred yawning.

Bill said, "Time to go inside, kid."

They went inside and washed up. With all the fresh air and excitement, Al fell asleep as soon as his head hit the pillow.

The morning light shone warmly into the cabin. Bill got up and got the stove going. Once done, he went outside and proceeded to the well. It was one of those old-time wells with a hand pump. He filled a pail, then returned to the cabin. Bill emptied the water into a tall jar, filling it halfway. The second pail Bill fetched filled the jar to the top with clean, fresh water. The jar had a spout near the bottom, which made filling a kettle for tea easy.

Al had just woken up. He watched his grandfather from the comfort of his bed.

Bill finally looked at Alfred's bed and smiled, "I can see you under the covers, boy, but now it's time to embrace the day the Lord has made."

Bill clapped his hands loudly and whistled as he poured water into a kettle.

Not used to 5 am wakeup, Alf yawned and slipped out of his covers. The cabin hadn't warmed up yet, so Alf quickly got out of his PJs and dressed. The old stove took its time heating the cabin but was hot enough for Bill to cook breakfast.

"Come on, Al, I've got hot porridge and tea," Bill announced.

Al got a bowl, filled it to the top, and then sat back down on his bed couch. Bill pointed to the small table at the end of Bill's bed. Alfred got the hint, moved to the table, and sat down.

Alfie commented on the pails of water Bill had brought up, which made him smile and laugh.

"What's so funny? Al asked.

"My boy, you'll bring the water in when you move here and wait till we have a bath." Still smiling, he added, "I hope you realize what you are getting into living out here with me. To live here takes a lot of work without any conveniences."

"Well, I must admit I'm not an early morning person," Al said as he scratched at his mop of hair.

"You are while you're staying with me, boy. When you come to live here and start bringing in the water daily, you'll get used to it and will be up and running at this time every day. You'll have to get your hair cut short before your final trip here, your new home. The less hair you have, the less hair you have to wash; Bill paused, and his face saddened.

He finally said, "I hope you'll like out here, son; so much work to do, Bill confessed. He stood up from his chair and started to clean up.

Al looked fondly at Bill and said, "Let me do this."

Bill smiled, "Help yourself, and thank you, Alfred."

The week went far too fast, and on the last day, Al started feeling sad. Bill noticed and reminded him to think about the good times we'll have in the future. After a walk, Bill invited Alfie to lose another game of checkers before he had to leave. He felt sorry for the young man and allowed him to win the game.

Alfred left for home around 11 am. He was power-walking when a man in a passing car stopped and asked if he needed a ride. Al jumped inside the car. The man was going to Bently. Alf thought that Jesus was indeed looking after him. He prayed silently and thanked Him for the ride home.

It was late afternoon when Alfie entered his house. Asleep on the couch lay his mother. He climbed the stairs to his bedroom. Grabbing a comic book, he sat on his bed. Alf could hear his brother's voice coming from Larry's room.

"Hey, toad breath, where have you been? Dad is mad at you. He wanted you to do something for him, and you weren't here," Larry said with a grin.

"I went to see granddad," Alfred answered as he tried to get comfortable on his lumpy mattress.

"How long have you been anyway?" Larry asked, without concern in his voice.

"All week," Alfie replied; he knew Larry wouldn't miss him.

"Why did you go and stay with that old kook? Larry jeered.

"He isn't a kook; he is very wise," Alfred said, putting his pillow over his head to drown out his brother's voice.

"Alfred, get down here now!" his dad commanded, "Where have you been? I needed you to help me fix the porch. I searched all over for you. I phoned Bert's place but got no answer. I finally gave up on the whole idea. The porch can fall apart if it wants to, as far as I'm concerned. Being unavailable when I needed you proves to me how useless you are, Alfred." Jake yelled as he left the house.

The rest of the day dwindled away. Al heard his father come home.

The family ate their meals when and where they wanted. Al grabbed his portion. Darlene was asleep on the couch as he returned to his room. Alf felt glad she was asleep. This way, he'd avoided being yelled at over something. Al was pretty tired. After he finished his pizza, he removed his clothes, crawled into bed, pulled back his covers, and fell asleep.

Morning came too soon as far as Alfie was concerned. Larry was already out of bed, making his presence known downstairs.

"Alfred's home Ma," Larry said with a dumb look.

Still on the couch, Darlene yelled upstairs with her usual raspy voice, "Get down here! You lazy kid."

Alfred put on his clothes, sat back on the bed, bent over, and tied his sockless shoes. He thought to himself and concluded that his mother didn't seem to have missed him either.

"We're out of bread," Larry announced as he ate the last piece. There was a half-eaten pizza a couple of days old in the fridge. Alfred grabbed a couple of pieces and left for school.

CHAPTER EIGHT

Paul Abandons Sabean

Proverbs 12:10

Whoever is righteous has regard for the life of his beast, but the mercy of the wicked is cruel.

"Go get it, girl," Michael yelled. Sabean caught the ball in mid-air, "Wow, way to go, Sabean." Mike encouraged as he bent down to take the ball away from her. His camouflage cap fell off, and Sabean took off with it in her mouth before he could grab it.

"Bring my cap back, you silly thing," Michael shouted.

The half-wolf ran fast around the backyard, with Mike following the best he could. On the third trip around, Sabean stopped. She stuck her rear in the air and shook the cap wildly in her mouth.

"Now come on, girl, don't wreck my cap," Mike pleaded.

Just as he approached the animal, Sabean took off around the yard again. After several round trips, Sabean dropped the cap and sat down with her tongue hanging out long as she panted heavily. Michael retrieved his cap; strangely enough, the cap had no damage and was still reasonably dry except for the rim. Mike inspected his cap and put it on again. Mike was happy his cap was okay and began stroking Sabean.

"Better put her on her leash, Michael. Dad will be home soon," Joyce called from the door.

Mike told Sabean how sorry he was, but it was time to go inside. He hooked the neck chain a little looser than it was, bent over, grabbed Sabean by the face, gave her a big kiss, and then went inside.

Summer seemed to have flown away, and now it was late September, and snow came down in drifts and drabs. The recently plowed roads made driving more accessible for the residents of Bently.

Paul drove into his driveway and noticed several male dogs in front of his fence.

"Get out of here!" Paul yelled at the dogs as he stepped out of his truck. He bent down, grabbed some rocks, and threw them at Sabean's admirers; the assorted suitors ran away.

He walked over to Sabean, unlatched the chain, and dragged her toward the trailer's shed by her neck.

"Come on, you useless cur. You're going into the shed till you're over this," Paul said as he dragged Sabean. Paul slammed the shed door shut and locked it.

"Mom, dad is putting Sabean in the shed," Michael said sadly.

"I know, but it's for her good; those dogs could hurt her," Joyce assured the boy.

"It's dark in the shed, and she'll be scared," Mike said with concern.

"Hush now; your dad is coming in," Joyce said softly.

Paul opened the door and announced. "Sabean has to go!" Paul said in a rage, then continued,

"She's in heat, and I won't put up with it again. Dogs of all sizes are whining and fighting. They've pooped all around the place in front of the gate!"

"Dad, she can't help it," begged Michael.

"Shut up! She's mine, and if I want to get rid of her, I will! This is the second time she's gone into heat, and I can't take it any longer, so I've locked her in the shed for now." Paul shouted.

Michael's face was red, and he began to cry.

"Shut up, Michael, and grow up! You're crying like a baby," Paul sneered in disgust.

Joyce put the supper on the table and sat down. Mike, still whimpering slightly, sat down too.

"Stop it, Michael; it will be okay," Joyce said softly.

Paul finished his meal, left the table, went into the living room, and picked up the phone.

"Hey, Brian, want to meet for a brewski or two?" Paul said, "Great, I'll see you at the bar."

Are you going out?" Joyce asked as her husband put on his jacket."

"Does it look like I am?" Paul sneered.

Joyce was tired and thought, I'm glad he's going out.

When Paul walked into the Black Spook Bar just outside Bently, Brian was already seated. He raised his hand, and Paul walked over to the table.

"How are you doing?" Brian said, smiling.

"Not good. That wolfdog of mine is in heat. Hey, are you looking for part wolf?" Paul asked.

"No way, man, that thing hates me," Brian answered, shaking his head.

"That's the problem; that beast hardly heeds me. I would shoot her, but I'll have the old lady and Mike crying." Paul thought.

Roman Knox sat down at their table, "How's it going, boys?"

"Hey, want to buy my part wolf?" Paul asked.

"No, thanks. I had to get rid of my dog already, so I don't need another problem," Roman said as he lit his cigarette.

"This is the second time I've come home to a bunch of dogs trying to get inside the gate," Paul said, shaking his head, then added, "When do dogs go into heat? It doesn't seem that long ago when she was in heat?"

Roman replied, "I think a dog can go into heat about every six months.

"How did you get rid of your dog?" Paul asked.

"I drove west about forty kms, stopped, pushed her out, and drove off. Why don't you take out that mutt of yours and drop her off there too?" Brian suggested.

"That's a good idea, pal. That way, I'll say she ran away." Paul smiled, adding, "I got her locked in the shed right now."

Roman's phone rang, and after a brief conversation, he stood up and announced he had to go.

"See ya," Brian said.

"I guess there isn't much hope of her surviving if she is more dog than wolf," Brian surmised.

"Frankly, I don't care," Paul replied.

Brian leaned forward and said in a low voice, "Tell Joyce you and I are going hunting ducks in the bush, and you want to take the dog. After all, it would be good for her to get out and run," Brian smiled, then said, "She'll think you are a great guy." Paul agreed.

"Yeah, and it isn't my fault that Sabean ran away. Let's do it next weekend."

"This is an excellent idea," Brian said.

"Let's take her out where Roman dropped off his dog. That should be far enough away just in case that stupid wolfdog decides to come home. Then we can spend the rest of the day at that new bar east of Bently." Paul summed up.

"Sounds like a plan." Brian nodded as he laid back in his seat.

The weekend finally came. Brian arrived at Paul's home early in the morning. He pounded on the door until Joyce opened it.

"Hi, Joyce. Is the old man ready to go?" questioned Brian.

Joyce entered the bedroom and announced, "Paul, Brian, is here."

Paul came into the kitchen with his rifle and a dog leash. Joyce didn't like Sabean going anywhere with Paul, especially since he was carrying a rifle. Her face expressed she was not happy.

Paul warned, "Don't give me that face. Sabean is mine. I told you, Joyce, that we were taking Sabean with us. It will do her good to run around all day."

"Yeh, a good romp in the bush would do her good, Joyce," Brian concurred.

The two men and Sabean left and got into Brian's van. They drove about forty km northwest, as Roman suggested. Arriving at Coates Lake, they stopped. They let Sabean out, then took out a couple of camp chairs and a cooler of beer. Sabean was having the time of her life. She could smell so many smells as she raced beside the lake bank.

"We might as well do a little hunting," Brian said.

"Yeh, we wouldn't want to lie to Joyce about going hunting?" Paul said, grinning.

Brian announced, "I think Coates Lake is a good place for fishing. We should camp here sometime and do a bit of fishing next summer."

"Spirit Lake is bigger and better fishing," Paul corrected, "Yeah, I'll take Joyce so she can cook and clean the fish; after all, what good is a wife unless she earns her keep," Paul smiled.

"Joyce won't mind that?" Brian asked.

"Too bad if she does. Anyway, the kid can play on the beach all day, and we will be free to fish, drink beer and have fun," Paul countered.

After a few hours, Paul and Brian started back to the van. They had shot a couple of ducks and felt pretty good about themselves. They packed up all their stuff and, without a thought, got in the van, turned the ignition on, and drove away.

Sabean found her way back to the van just as Brian and Paul began to drive down the gravel road. Sabean panicked and began to chase the car. Poor Sabean ran until she couldn't run anymore. Exhausted from the chase, the animal stopped and found a resting place. Hours went by, and still, the van didn't return. The next day she went on the highway and tried to stop cars by standing on the pavement. Fortunately, people stopped long enough for Sabean to see if Joyce or Michael were in their car. However, a big grey gravel truck barreled down the highway and almost hit her, stopping her investigation. A dirt path veered off the highway and looked safer. She wandered down the path until she found the remains of a dead deer; there was still a bit of meat left on the carcass.

Torn flesh alerted Sabean's senses. Three pesky crows on the remains stood their ground arrogantly. Sabean lunged in and ate her fill with a chorus of loud caws from the disgruntled crows until she felt full. Fully satisfied, she walked into the bush. It wasn't long before Sabean encountered a dog's skeleton, someone had probably abandoned. She sniffed it, then wandered off. Sabean spotted an evergreen tree with long boughs like the tree at home. She worked her way beneath the boughs and settled down for a sleep. Even though she was often abused and chained to a big tree, it was the only home Sabean knew. She thought of Michael and whimpered a bit. Sabean was a survivor, and her wolf blood seemed to dominate. She would survive the winter ahead better than most abandoned animals that couldn't fend for themselves.

Sabean had never experienced freedom like this before, but she felt sad. Even though her master was less than kind, she had always had a home. She could hear the howls of the wolves in the far-off hills. Their howls were much louder where Sabean was now. Instinctually, she wanted to return the call but instead let out a low moan. The wolf symphony continued, and finally, Sabean chorused in.

Morning came, and the sun was rising when Sabean woke. She scratched her neck vigorously where the neck chain had been for so long. She was still filled with last night's feast but felt strangely hungry. Michael always fed her in the morning. Sabean felt sad as she thought of Michael. She laid her head back down. Her ears perked up at the sound of rustling. She smelt something, then followed her nose. It's a mouse making its way through the brush. Instinct kicked in, and Sabean was on the rodent in a split second. It did little to help her hunger but satisfied her need to survive. Walking a bit more, she encountered another mouse that ran right in front of her. Sabean tried to catch him, but she wasn't fast enough this time, and the mouse got away.

A few days passed, and Sabean's hunting skills still had not improved. She heard a noise from a stand of poplar trees. She had learned to approach her prey with a bit more finesse. Closing in on the sound, she smelt the familiar mouse smell. The wolfdog's ears perked up, and once her eyes spotted the rodent's location, she pounced quickly and got it.

Sabean kept her hunting area small and in a circle to be on the safe side. She was happy to end her safety circle at Spirit Lake's shoreline. The ice began to form at the lake's edge, but water still ran freely. She drank the water eagerly. Refreshed by the cold drink, she began to hunt again. The sun had reached high noon, and the heat felt warm on her thick coat. As night approached, Sabean retreated under her evergreen and fell into a deep sleep.

Sabean awoke to the sounds of hooves on the ground right next to her hideout. Five deer were munching on some remaining greenery. Sabean's body exploded out of her under-tree den. She made quite a lot of noise in the process, which scared the deer off. After a chase, Sabean stopped, and her stomach grumbled at her loss. She surveyed the area and saw a pair of large ears yards away. Trying to be quiet, she crept through the grass. The rabbit saw her and tried to run down a hole, but Sabean's long nose poked down the hole and caught him. He was a large rabbit that almost afforded his freedom by racking Sabean's nose heavily with its claws and powerful back legs. Suddenly, the rodent twisted itself and scratched Sabean's face and side. Even though her side and nose hurt badly, Sabean hung onto him tightly. The smell of blood made her bite even harder, and at last, she subdued the rodent. The blood from her nose ran down her face. Sabean ate and felt better. She walked through the bush for the rest of the day, hoping to see another unfortunate rodent for dessert. The sun started to disappear behind the hills as night approached. The wind was cold and blew hard against Sabean's body as she returned under the broad boughs of her evergreen. Sabean dug out a nice groove in the ground, which fit her body nicely. It was just deep enough for her to snuggle down, and any breeze that managed to sneak under the tree's branches was now limited. Sabean licked at her wounds. It wasn't long before she fell asleep.

CHAPTER NINE

Paul Returns Without Sabean

Paul returned home late at night. He slept soundly until morning.

"Get me some coffee Joyce," Paul yelled from the bathroom.

Joyce put the coffee together, then entered the living room where Paul was sitting.

"Did you get any ducks?" Joyce asked.

"Brian got a couple of ducks; what's it to you." He answered.

"Just curious, Paul, that's all," she replied.

Paul got up, followed Joyce into the kitchen, and accused her of sitting around doing nothing while he risked his life to put supper on the table.

"No, I gave the place a good cleaning, and Betty came over for a bit," Joyce said.

"Oh yeah, I bet you spent the afternoon gossiping about everyone," Paul retorted.

"Paul, I don't do that, and by the way, where is Sabean?"

"Watch your tone, lady," Paul said, staring intently at Joyce, then placing his mouth right next to her ear; he yelled, "She ran away!"

"What do you mean she ran away," Joyce asked, holding her hand over her ear.

Paul swatted her across the face, "Paul, stop it!" Joyce pleaded.

Michael could hear the commotion in the other room and feared for his mom.

"Please don't hurt her," he said softly to himself.

Noise from the kitchen continued until the sound of the back door slammed shut. Michael came out and found his mother crying on a chair.

"Mom, are you okay?" Mike asked with a higher-than-usual voice.

"I'll be okay, son. For now, dear, just go back to your room," Joyce said weakly. A few minutes passed, and Mike needed to be with his mom, so he returned to the kitchen.

"I'm much better now, son," Joyce told her son as she swept the floor with a forced grin on her tear-stained face.

"Michael, I have something to tell you," Joyce said, dreading his response, then continued,

"I think you better sit down." Joyce put her hand on his and said, "Sabean took off and ran away somewhere. Dad couldn't find her."

Michael's face dropped, "I thought maybe he had put her back in the shed," Mike said with quivering lips.

Paul's truck drove back into the driveway. The lock turned, and the door swung open.

"Where's my wallet?" Paul bellowed.

"I think it's on the coffee table," Joyce answered.

Michael yelled, "What happened to Sabean?"

"She ran off, and don't you talk to me that way, kid," Paul warned.

"You killed her, didn't you? I hate you!" Mike yelled.

The boy fell as Paul cuffed the side of his head hard. Joyce ran over and picked her son up.

"Leave him alone, Paul, or I'll," Joyce said.

"You'll what? That little brat disrespected me and got what's coming to him." Paul said with a face like a thundercloud.

With tears in his eyes, Mike held onto his mother's side. "Get in your room before I really give it to you," Paul shouted as he turned to leave.

The phone rang, and it was Betty.

"He hit Michael, Betty, and had I not been here, I would hate to think what he might have done to him. I don't know what to do." Joyce cried.

"I'll be there as soon as possible, my friend," Betty responded.

Five minutes later, Betty arrived. Joyce opened the door to find Betty with her arms spread wide to hug her friend.

"It will all work out, my dear friend," Betty said while rubbing Joy's back in tender circles.

Michael approached the women, and Betty leaned down and hugged the boy. Joyce motioned everyone to sit at the kitchen table. Joy felt much better now that Betty had arrived. She smiled and said, "You're such a good friend, Betty.

Paul's truck came to a skidding stop in the driveway again. The door flew open. Paul stood there with anger written all over his face.

"What are you doing here, Betty?" Paul shouted.

"Comforting your wife and child," Betty snapped back defiantly.

The box of Mike's toy cars fell off the counter.

"Now, look at what you've done, you dumb kid," Paul said, shaking his head in disgust.

Mike ran over and started to pick up the cars when his father walked toward him. Paul stumbled on one of the small toys and fell hard onto his knees. Paul's face was red from anger when he finally got to his feet.

"What are you doing with all this garbage all over the floor," Paul yelled.

"It just fell off the counter," Michael replied with a frightened face.

"You stupid kid, you just about broke my legs with your toys everywhere," Paul screamed.

He hit the side of Mike's head with the back of his hand. The young boy flew sideways from the impact. Joyce ran from the kitchen, shouting, "Leave him alone!"

Betty stood by Joy. Paul grabbed Joyce, threw her against the wall, and slapped her violently. Betty and Mike tried to pull Paul off of her. Paul's body seemed to vibrate with anger as he gave his wife one final strike while pushing Betty and Mike away. He picked up a bag from his chair and left. Paul's truck roared as he spun his tires, then left his yard, and without looking, he approached the street. Paul sideswiped a car driving by. The car and the truck seemed to spin around from the impact. Jim Jordon managed to get out of the driver's side of his car. The back end of his car was completely smashed in and looked like a write-off. Brused and in shock, Mr. Jordon went to the truck and looked inside. Paul's bloodied face was all he could see. He tried to talk to Paul, but he wasn't responding. Joyce heard the crash and went outside. Jim yelled at Joyce to phone 911, which she did.

Paul had regained consciousness by the time the ambulance arrived, but blood still poured over his face from a head wound. The police arrived and began to try to make sense of what had happened. Jim attempted to explain over Paul's loud, angry voice. Paul kept accusing Jim of not watching where he was going.

Jim explained, "I was driving along going east when that truck slammed hard into the back end of my car."

As the police checked the evidence, they surmised it was Paul's fault and told him so. Paul wouldn't hear of it and kept swearing and being belligerent. The ambulance arrived. They loaded Paul into the ambulance.

The policeman, Bernie Lehman, shouted at Joyce, "Are you the one who called in the accident?"

"Yes," Joyce answered.

Betty hugged Joy, and Mike stayed close to his mom. Officer Lehman approached Joyce. He could see her face was red and swollen.

"Were you in the truck?" asked Bernie.

"No, the man in the truck is my husband," Joyce said.

Joyce was aware of the policeman's face as he looked at her closely.

"What is your name, and what happened to you." the officer asked. Michael began crying. Mike's face showed a welp mark.

"My name is Joyce Ross, and this is my son, Michael," she said with an unsettled look.

"What happened here?" Bernie asked with authority.

Joyce, Mike, Betty, and Bernie went inside. Joyce explained that Paul had a temper, got himself upset, and left in his truck angry.

"Did he hit you?" Bernie inquired, "Do you want to press charges, Mrs. Ross?"

"No, it will just make matters worse. Let's leave it," Joyce said apologetically.

"I can't make you press charges, but I think I will talk to your husband. He's in a lot of trouble," Bernie said, then walked to his cruiser.

Officer Lehman joined his partner Officer Leask in the squad car and followed the ambulance. Arriving at the hospital, the two policemen waited to see what the doctor had to say about Paul's injury and whether he thought there was any permanent damage. The Emergency room doctor said Paul had a slight concussion, but except for some stitches, he could leave.

Bernie made his way to Paul's hospital bed but passed by it. He stared out of the window.

Paul asked defiantly, "Have you charged that other guy yet?" as he sat up.

Officer Lehman ignored him. Bernie's actions infuriated Paul. He got out of bed, came up behind him, and tried to punch him just as Bernie turned around. He grabbed Paul with his vice-gripped hands, backed him up to his bed, and threw him down on it.

"You can't grab me like that." Paul said, "I have rights. Did you charge that other guy yet?"

No, but I'm charging you with undue care and attention, causing an accident, assaulting an officer, and domestic abuse, if I had my way. I think you better come with me down to the station," Bernie said without waiting for Paul's response.

He took Paul by the arm, grabbed the other, and cuffed him. Bernie guided Paul with the handcuffs and the back of his neck collar into the squad car. Still angry and thinking about the marks on Joyce and the welp on the young boy's face, he was tempted not to place his hand on Paul's head as he entered the police car, but he refrained. Paul just kept on swearing as he sat in the back seat.

Joyce spent the day with Betty, waiting to hear word back from Officer Lehman about Paul.

The phone rang, and Joyce said, "Oh, Betty, they're charging Paul with reckless driving involving an accident.

"I think you should charge him with assault," Betty said.

"Betty, you know it will just worsen things, and he could likely come home and give me another beating. I'm his wife, and I married him for better or for worse, but I didn't think it could get this bad." Joyce explained and said, "It's mainly my fault, Betty. I shouldn't have married a non-Christian. God warns us about that." Joyce defended.

"Everyone makes mistakes, but you and Michael can't go on like this, my dear friend," Betty advised.

"I won't have him hurt, Michael. I'm setting down some strict rules when Paul gets home. I'll threaten to leave him if he hurts Mike again," Joyce said between tears.

"Didn't you say he would kill you if you left him?" Betty asked.

"I know, I know, oh, I just don't know what to do," Joyce said, then put her hands over her face and cried heavily.

Betty said, "You have a defender in Christ; in 2 Thessalonians 1, verse six, He will pay back trouble to those who trouble you. How's that for quoting the Bible, Joy?"

"Good," Joyce said.

Joy shook her head and confessed, "You know, usually, I wouldn't wish Paul trouble, but I have lost so much respect for him since I saw him hit Michael." Joy's face looked exhausted.

Betty confessed that she wasn't as knowledgeable about the Bible as Joy was. Still, she had been reading her Bible daily for a couple of weeks seeking advice about her problems and Joyce's. Betty was worried for Joy and Michael.

Betty relayed, "I started looking in the Bible to see what God has said regarding husbands and wives. "When you married Paul, you made a covenant with him. You two became one flesh. You both made oaths, but only one of you has kept theirs. God has said in Ephesians 5:25: Husbands love your wives, just as Christ loved the church. He has broken his promise to you and God.

Joyce sat down, stared at the floor, and contemplated Betty's words. Betty put her arm around her and comforted her.

"I can't have Paul hitting Michael again, so I will consider what you've said, Betty, unless God tells me differently. I will always love the man I married deep down, Betty, but unless

Paul makes significant changes toward Michael and me, I might have to leave him and take my chances," Joyce said.

CHAPTER TEN

Al and Bert Drive to See Bill

It was a Saturday, and Alfred was looking out the kitchen window when Bert appeared in his van, alone without his dad. Beep-Beep sounded the horn as Bert drove up with his window down and an ear-to-ear grin. Alf grabbed his jacket and went to the window of the van.

"Where's your dad?" Al asked.

"At home, dad said I'm okay to drive on my own, and I have an idea I think you'll like. Let's visit your granddad. My van needs some highway driving to blow out the cobwebs," Bert suggested.

"Wow, I would love that," Alfred said with enthusiasm. Al jumped into the van, and off they went. They turned off the highway onto a gravel road. A 'Beware of Wildlife' sign came into view. Al cautioned Bert to slow down.

"Now, pull over to the side and park right after you see the sign for the campground. I'm afraid it's on foot from here through a bushy trail," Al warned.

Bert parked safely on the side of the road, got out, and locked up. They walked across the road to a trail. It wasn't long before they encountered what Al called granddad's defense line. Wild rose bushes with spiny prickles stood guard here and there down the trail. Alf prepared for the hazards, grabbed a stick, and bent around the prickly bushes. Bert walked carefully to avoid falling into holes in the trail's uneven terrain. He diligently surveyed the ground. He wasn't looking ahead and walked headlong into a large wild rose bush.

"Ouch! Al, please help me. I'm all caught up in this bush!" Bert yelled.

Alfred turned, slowly pulled Bert away from the offending prickles, and told him to expect more. Bert made it through the rest of the trail with only minor scratches.

"I'm going to see if granddad has a machete so I can clear this trail. I think he must not clear it very often." Alf said.

The boys walked to the cabin and knocked on the door; no one answered.

"He must be checking his traps or something, so let's sit on the steps until he returns," Al proposed.

They wore warm clothes and were happy they did. They waited about ten minutes before seeing Bill walking from a trail that joined the campground next door.

"Hi, I missed you so much I had to see you; my friend drove me here," Al put his arm around Bert and continued, "Granddad, this is my best friend, Bert."

Bill smiled and shook Bert's hand.

"Nice to meet you, Alfred's best friend Bert," Bill said, smiling.

"Nice to meet you, sir," Bert replied.

"Best friend and good manners, too," Bill commented, "Come inside, and I'll make you boys some tea."

The boys sat on the couch while Bill put the kettle on.

"We can only stay for the day." Al conveyed.

"Well, that's better than nothing. The next time you two come, expect to stay at least overnight," Bill insisted, "I think I still have an air mattress in the shed. By the way, "where did you park your car?"

"We parked it on the side of the road and came through the trail over there like I did the last time." Alf pointed out the window toward the bushy trail they came in on.

"Well, next time, turn onto the campground road, which will take you right up to that short trail across from my cabin." Bill pointed straight ahead.

"Oh dear, I'm sorry. I think I have the old trail on the map I gave you, Alfred. I established this new trail to get to the campground quicker. The owner has hired me to look after the campground. I was checking on things over there when you must have arrived." Bill declared.

The day went fine; they all got along well. Bert announced he needed a bathroom, so Bill told him how to get to it. Bert found the outhouse easily in the daylight.

Alfred said, "Bert, try remembering the way to the outhouse because it's hard to see at night. Some sturdy sticks with fluorescent paint along the pathway make things easier to see when it's dark."

"Okay," Bert said, thinking he would watch for thorny bushes and the ground's surface as he made his way. He found the trail easy to follow and said so when he returned.

"Granddad, you should have seen Bert all caught up in a monster rose bush on your old trail. I had to pull him off; his hair was all tangled in the prickles," Alf explained through fits of laughter.

"Ah, come on, it wasn't that funny," Bert defended, grinning.

Bert was intrigued by everything Bill said and did. He thought it amazing that the old guy built the cabin and sheds himself.

Bill asked. "Want to learn about the land? God provides almost everything a guy needs to stay alive."

"That would be very interesting, Mr. Dennis," Bert replied.

Bill picked up a long stick to use as a walking stick, which also came in handy to clear the brush as they explored some not-so-traveled paths.

"God provides," Bill stated as they came across some wild herbs, one of which was yarrow.

Bill suggested, "Always try to feel and smell plants, and that way, you can tell most times what they are good for."

The young man felt the plant, then smelled it and said, "Smells a little bit like sage."

The old man explained, "This is an excellent plant for many things like fever, common colds, hay fever, diarrhea, loss of appetite, and gas discomfort. Some people chew the fresh leaves to relieve toothache. Drink this as a tea with some wild raspberry leaves and some wild mint, which will help you feel better. You have to button up and stay warm, though, because I find yarrow makes me sweat a bit, which is good to do if you got a cold. Just stay warm."

As the two traveled on, Bill pointed out many plants with edible and medicinal properties. He told them that the common dandelion is a good tonic and diuretic for infections and digestive symptoms, and the roasted root is a good coffee substitute." Bill informed. He stopped at a bunch of nettle plants, "Be careful when picking them because they can leave a nasty sting on your fingers. I cut them from the bottom, hang them upside down with gloves, and let them dry. Once they are dry, they don't sting you. I make tea with nettles and add mint. This plant is one of the best plants because it will give you iron and is easy to digest. I throw it in many meals. Wild rose leaves are good in a salad as well as the flowers. The fruit of wild strawberries and raspberries is so tasty, but you must be prepared to pick a long time to get enough for jam; I think it is worth the time it takes, though," Bill informed.

They seemed only to walk a few steps, and the old fellow would explain the next plant they encountered. Bill said he dries the herbs and keeps them in big jars a restaurant gave him. Finally, they found a clear patch of grass and sat down. They enjoyed the symphony of the forest and the creature sounds. The sun was starting to go down.

"Come on, kids, let's head for my cabin," Bill said as he got up. He patted both boys on the back to encourage them along. The day went by quickly. Bert had to be home by 6 pm.

"Thank you very much, Bert, for driving Alfred here, and please feel free to visit me any time you like, Bert; any friend of my grandson is a friend of mine," he stated.

Bill asked if he could have Bert's phone number so they could all get together somewhere when he was in town getting supplies.

"Bert said as he took a pen from his pocket. "What a great idea; call me, and I will drive you back unless I'm away, Mr. Dennis."

Bill gave him a piece of paper; Bert handed it back with his contact information.

"It's been a terrific day, but we must leave," Alfred said.

"You have made me so happy, and I look forward to seeing you guys again soon," Bill expressed.

The boys started to leave by the way they came.

"Stop, go through that short trail to the campground instead, then walk down the path to your vehicle; I think you'll find it less painful, Bert," Bill said, smiling.

"Thank you," Al said as they walked to the shorter trail.

Their visit uplifted Bill. He started thinking how nice it would be if he could somehow have a place for Bert to sleep over the next time they were out.

CHAPTER ELEVEN

Bill Makes Room For Bert

Bill started to think about how he could accommodate Bert with a place to sleep the next time they came for a visit. He looked for the air mattress in the shed, but it had holes. Bill dragged it to the campground's big garbage bin. As he returned home, he felt terrible for leaving the air mattress in the shed for years deteriorating it. "Oh my, how the time flies," Bill thought.

The old man entered his cabin and poured himself a cup of tea, then sat down outside on his rocker. He thought about how to make a bed for Bert. His cabin was only so wide, and there wasn't any room left. He scratched his head and then prayed. It wasn't long before an idea came to him. If the cabin isn't wide enough, then he'd build up.

As he often did, he talked to himself out loud, "I'll build a bunk bed frame over the couch. It will be slightly higher than usual so people can still sit on the couch without hitting their heads. I'll have to make a ladder so Bert can reach his bunk; yes, that's the answer."

He decided to get the wood he'd need and start first thing in the morning. Bill was excited about the plan, stood up, and did a joyful jig.

The next day the man walked behind his cabin, past the outhouse, and traveled through the bush. A semblance of an old trail led him to where an old run-down house was. He had grown up in it and brought Darlene up there, too. Bill had taken most of the good lumber from the old house to build his cabin and sheds, but he hoped a few good pieces were left. The old timer rummaged through the lumber, and a nice piece of plywood with a rough end came into sight; he also found some strong 2x4s. He had to make a few exhausting trips back to his cabin with all the wood he would need to build the bunk bed, but he did it joyfully.

Bill went inside one of the sheds, brought out a hammer, a saw, and a bag of nails, and placed them on the porch. The old boy sat down on his rocking chair and thought about how he would construct the bunk bed using the couch as the bottom bunk. Bill put the whole thing together in his mind. He prayed that Jesus would supervise him to build it solid and safe. Bill worked on the frame for the rest of the day, but his aging muscles told him to stop and finish the job tomorrow.

After a good restful sleep, Bill started working on the project right after breakfast. He never had any carpentry schooling, but he seemed to be a natural at building things. He worked on the project all day until completion. The old fellow grabbed the frame and tried to see if it shook; it was solid. He picked up the plywood and sawed off a small bit of uneven wood while downsizing it to fit the bottom of the new upper bed. Laying down his hammer, Bill poured a cup of tea, sat down, and admired the job. It was a little odd-looking, but it would do nicely. He just needed to figure out how to get a mattress, some sheets, and a blanket to complete it. He prayed about it and knew Jesus would come through.

Mr. Tom Taylor owned the campground beside Bill's property. He approached Bill a few years back and asked if he would be interested in keeping an eye on the place and collecting the camping fees. Bill told him that would be no problem. He kept the money safely in his cellar. Tom had a small windowless building at the campsite with a phone inside, which was locked tight. He entrusted Bill with the key just in case there was a problem.

Tom decided to drive to his campground and see how things were. He parked his truck by the small building and got out.

"Hey Bill, I can see you've been on the job." declared Tom.

"Yeh, I check every day in the spring, summer, and fall but only occasionally in the winter," Bill replied.

"I think I'd better pay you more," Tom conveyed.

"Oh, that's okay; I like having a job. Say, by the way, Tom, I've built a bunk bed over the couch, and I need a clean mattress and some bedding; if you come across those items on your travels, perhaps you could bring them to me the next you come out? Just take what it costs from my pay, if that's okay?" Bill asked, hoping.

"It's funny you would ask that because I'm staying overnight at my parent's place, and they have a gently used mattress they want to get rid of, and I'm sure she'll have some bedding. My mom never seems to throw things of usefulness out. She keeps everything, but lately, she is starting to downsize. Hey, do you know what else they have?

Bill, can you ride a bike because they're giving one away? I looked at it, and it's in pretty good shape." Tom informed.

"Well, it's been a long time since I rode a bike, but I bet my grandson would appreciate it, especially when he moves in with me. It would give him freedom from being with this old guy, day in and day out," Bill perceived.

Tom asked, "Your grandson is coming to live with you?"

"Alfred will probably be without a home next June, so I invited him here. He's had a tough life at home and needs someone to love and guide him. Plus, I'm getting on in years, so having a young, strong fellow to help around here would make my life a whole lot easier, not to mention I'll have company. Being alone is getting to me a bit, especially in the winter. I feel Alfred is God-sent," Bill explained.

Bill invited Tom for lunch. Tom gratefully accepted. He offered Tom some of his wild tea. Tom accepted. Bill filled Tom's cup and placed it on the table. He also gave Tom a small pouch filled with the same tea.

"Thanks, Bill, your tea is excellent. I feel that your tea cured a nasty cold I had.

"I'm going back to mom's tonight, so I'll bring the bedding and the bike out tomorrow morning before I drive back to my place," Tom said with a warm smile on his clean, shaven face.

Bill voiced concern. "God bless you, Tom, but I don't expect you to drive all the way back here tomorrow just for me."

"It would be my pleasure. What's thirty-four km anyway," responded Tom.

"A long way if you're walking." Bill laughed.

"You mean to tell me you walk all the way to Bently? Tom inquired.

"Yes, for my supplies. I sometimes get a ride, but sometimes I don't." Bill affirmed.

"You're an incredible man, Bill. I've got a couple of things I want to do, and then I'll see you tomorrow," Tom assured him.

"When you come back, do you want to stay for lunch again, Tom? I'll have some nice rabbit stew if you're interested," Bill invited.

Tom smiled and said, "That would be nice, and consider that as payment for my gas. I'm getting the mattress, bedding, and bike free, so you don't owe me anything."

"Well, then I'll have some bannock ready for you too. I love to have a dinner companion Tom; I can't thank you enough," the old man said sincerely.

Bill bid Tom goodbye and then whistled a tune to himself.

"Wow! My dear Jesus, that was a fast answer to prayer; thank you," Bill prayed. The elderly man put together a pot of rabbit stew and made some bannock. He was so grateful to God for once again coming to his aid.

Around noon the following day, Bill could hear Tom's truck. It wasn't long before Tom came up to the cabin.

"Smells good," Tom complemented as he walked up the steps and through the opened door.

"Come on in, Tom. Everything is ready." Bill invited.

"Actually, why don't you help me with the mattress and bedding first?" Tom suggested.

Bill and Tom brought over the mattress and bedding. Tom climbed the ladder to reach the top bunk. Bill handed

Tom the top of the mattress while he held the bottom part; once that was up, he handed him the bedding.

"Just put the bedding on the mattress, Tom. I can make the bed up later," Bill said.

The two men ate their lunch; they enjoyed their conversations until it started to get late.

Tom reluctantly stood up and announced he had to go. "Let me show you the bike," Tom said as he descended the stairs.

Seeing the bike, Bill gratefully said. "It's in real good shape, Tom. Thank you for everything you've done and have done over the years."

After Tom left, Bill climbed the bunk bed ladder, folded the bedding neatly, and put them in a bag. He put the bag under the mattress so the bedding would stay clean. He would only have to wipe the mattress down when needed.

Bill thought aloud, "I hope Bert isn't afraid of heights."

CHAPTER TWELVE

Paul Goes to Jail

Paul spent time in Dean Remand Centre, about 10 km. from Bently, till his court date. While there, his mouth got him in big trouble. Jim, a large inmate, disliked Paul and told him to know his place or he'd pay. Paul laughed and went to walk away. Jim grabbed Paul by the back of his neck and laid a beating on him. Paul tried to fight back but learned he had mouthed off to the wrong guy.

Jim had found out that Paul pushed his wife around through the grapevine; this information fueled his hatred toward Paul. It seemed everything Paul did infuriate him. One day when there was no one in the laundry room except Paul, Jim decided to teach Paul how it felt to be small and incapable of defending himself. Big Jim told Paul he was about to feel what it was like to be Mrs. Ross. The big guy punched Paul so hard that he fell backward. He couldn't get to his feet and lay face up on the floor, somewhat dazed. A guard heard the commotion and proceeded to the laundry room. Jim could hear the guard's footsteps coming and quickly leaned over Paul shaking his fist, and told him, "Say nothing, or I'll give you some more."

Jim escaped by a door that adjoined the kitchen. The guard came in and saw Paul on the floor and asked, "What's going on here?"

Paul managed to sit up and said he had slipped and fallen. The guard helped him up and took him to the infirmary. A doctor cleaned him up and kept him overnight for observation. The next day, Paul was led back to his cell by a guard who displayed no compassion for his pain and his badly bruised face.

Pastor Josh visited the prison every couple of weeks. He heard about a man just released from the infirmary and returned to his cell. The pastor had a guard show him to Paul's cell. He visited Paul often while Paul was awaiting his psychiatric assessment and court appearance. After their many conversations, Paul dedicated himself to Jesus.

Finally, his day in court arrived. The judge suspended his license and gave him 100 hours of community work. Around 4 o'clock, Paul was released.

Pastor Josh went to see Joyce before Paul's release. He had a long talk with her about Paul. He explained that the assessment showed Paul has significant anger issues, requiring him to see a professional as part of the court's ruling.

The Pastor said, "It may be easier for Paul to control himself if we get to the bottom of that anger. Joyce, you must be firm with Paul because his main trigger is alcohol; or you're asking to see his anger emerge. Your husband has a significant alcohol dependence that I feel has affected his mind. I've seen this before with some people who have drunk heavily for a long time. They can never seem to drink only one or two drinks. They drink to get drunk; they like the high, which can lead to permanent brain damage over time in some. Paul has had time to dry out, and I am happy to say he has dedicated his life to Jesus. Joyce, this is wonderful, but I want you to be aware of the trials you might face with Paul. He's all excited about reuniting with you and Michael. I hope Paul won't give in to his sinful nature or the enemy's whispers and go back to drinking as time passes. I worry that Satan will make Paul's life as challenging as possible, so expect frustration in many forms as he fights to stay sober Joyce. Paul is blessed to have such a wonderful Christian wife. Let's hope your godly attitude will help encourage him to hang on."

Pastor Josh placed his hand tenderly on Joyce's shoulder and said, "Take good care of yourself and your son. I must go now, but here's my phone number if you ever need to talk. Goodbye Joyce and God bless."

The Pastor no sooner left when a cab drove up, and Paul got out. Joyce sent Michael into the safety of his room. Even with the encouraging words the Pastor gave, Joyce was still waiting for the worse to happen. She was surprised to see Paul come in, place his coat on the hanger, and ask her if they could sit down and talk. Paul sat for a moment, then looked Joyce in her eyes and confessed he was a lousy husband and father. Paul reached out and held Joy's hands softly and said, "Joyce, I have been horrible to you, and if you let me, I would like to try to be a better husband and father to our son," Paul said with commitment in his voice then added, "I have asked Jesus into my heart, and he has forgiven me. Will you forgive me, Joyce?"

Joyce was flabbergasted. It felt like a dream had come true. Paul stood up, as did Joy. She stood on her tiptoes, put her arms around Paul's neck, and said, "I forgive you, my darling."

Paul said, "Pastor Josh has been such a tremendous inspiration to me. He pointed out that if I start thinking about drinking, I should remember that liquor is my enemy and isn't a part of my new life with Christ. Joyce told Paul how proud she was of him.

Over the next few days, Paul seemed to be a different man. He often invited Mike to a game of ball. While playing ball, Paul noticed the chain Sabine wore and became convicted of his cruelty. Joyce was pleased to see Paul's new nature and noted he hadn't called his drinking pals to avoid temptation.

At night the Ross family sat on the couch watching TV together. Joyce snuggled between Paul and Michael. She had dreamed of enjoying themselves like this and thought this family would be okay after all. Her mind periodically played a couple of scenarios that had nagged her since Paul came home. Joyce would be making dinner or something when suddenly her thoughts played scenes of how things were before Paul's commitment to Christ, which frightened her, then she would remind herself that Paul would have to depend strongly on Jesus to keep him straight.

After a few weeks, Joyce saw her husband having a few minor outbursts of anger, but Paul would eventually settle down and say he was sorry. Joyce thought maybe they should go somewhere to break the monotony. She knew Paul and the family loved to camp at Spirit Lake, which would allow Paul to relax and go fishing. Joyce began to make plans.

Joyce suggested to Paul and Mike the following day, "Why don't we go to Spirit Lake and camp for a couple of days? Wouldn't that be fun?"

Michael let out a shriek of excitement and jumped off the couch. Joyce grabbed Paul, gave him a loving hug, and with a grin, said, "doesn't that sound fun, dear?" Paul's face brightened up, and he agreed.

The following weekend the Ross family packed and were on their way to enjoy each other near the lake. Paul rented a rowboat and went fishing. While he was gone, an old fellow who lived next to the campground dropped around; he asked how Joy was doing. Joyce invited him to sit down and have some iced tea. Old Bill and Joyce began talking about the Lord and got along famously. The old guy had some chores, so he bid Joyce goodbye.

The weekend went by fast, and it was time to go home. Although Joy could see Paul was getting a bit hyper near the end of the weekend, they still had a good time. Paul was very quiet but claimed he was all right on the drive home. Once home, Joy unpacked, and she could feel something had changed in Paul since they left.

Things had been beautiful around the Ross home for almost a month, but Paul now seemed depressed and became more easily upset as the days passed. Joyce tried to make excuses for him in her mind, but she could see her husband was going downhill. Paul started watching TV from his chair rather than cuddling up with the family on the couch. Hour after hour would go by, and Paul wouldn't talk. Joyce asked him if he was okay, and he claimed he was until one day, she asked again, only to see Paul fly off the handle.

"Why can't everybody just leave me alone?" Paul shouted, "How would you feel if all your friends stopped coming around? I'm tired of water, tea, and juice and bored to death being around here. I need some time to myself."

Joyce's heart fell. She entered the kitchen and sat at the table to process what was happening. She felt she was losing her husband and the friendship she thought they had developed. Joyce prayed.

CHAPTER THIRTEEN

Bert and Alfie Go To Bill's at Christmas

The Christmas shows on TV told stories about happy families at Christmas. They made Alfred very sad. There was no resemblance to that kind of closeness in his family except for Alf's grandfather. He couldn't get him off his mind; Al thought how lonely it would be for him this time of the year.

Bert and his parents were concerned for Bill Dennis too. Mr. Black suggested that Bert could take Alfred to see his grandfather since they've had a mild winter and the roads are good.

"Wow, that's a great idea!" Bert exclaimed.

Virginia said. "I would like to send you up there with some baking. I think I'll put the baked goods in containers, wrap them up in Christmas paper, and put them inside a box."

"I'll call Alf and give him the good news," Bert said, grinning as he picked up the phone,

"Hi man, what's up?" Al queried.

Bert exclaimed, "What does Mr. Dennis do at Christmas?

"Gosh, I don't really know." Al guessed.

"My mom was thinking about him. My parents enjoy hearing you talk about your granddad and all his accomplishments and stories, so mom decided to do some Christmas baking for him. Also, I have a little money and thought we could buy him a present for Christmas," Bert suggested.

Alf's face lit up, and he confessed in a low voice that he'd been getting up early Fridays and Saturdays after the bar closed and picked-up beer cans and bottles. He had managed to save $15.30 so far."

"That's great because we can get something nice if we put our money together," Bert surmised.

"I would love to go and see him," Al said with excitement.

"I'll pick you up, and let's see what Jack Snacks has in the way of Christmas gifts," Bert suggested.

It wasn't long before Al saw his friend drive up; Alfred ran outside and got into the van. As they entered Jack's, the smell of Patchouli oil was extra apparent. There were some reasonably priced sweaters, shirts, and socks; the boys stopped to look them over. Bert picked a warm-looking brown sweater and some batteries for the tree lights. Alf picked a pair of thick brown socks. Happy with their purchases, they returned to Bert's to pick up the baking. Virginia told them to wait while she wrapped the socks and sweater. She picked out a beautiful Christmas card with a sparkly snow scene on the front and wrote a lovely Bible verse inside. They put the items in a box and were about to leave when Bert's mom handed them another box; it contained a small imitation Christmas tree with lights that ran on batteries.

"Oh, I remember that tree; you used to put it in my room when I was little." Bert reminisced.

That's right, and it's a shame to store it away when I'm sure your grandfather would appreciate it," Virginia remarked.

"Mrs. Black, thank you for the tree and all your baking. I can't wait to see my granddad's face when we give all this to him," Alfred said with sincerity.

The two boys laughed and talked on the way up to Bill's.

. As Bill got older, he became pretty lonely in the winter months. Days without human companionship took their toll, especially around Christmas. Thanks to Tom, Bill had all the supplies he needed because Tom drove him for supplies in November. The old fellow thought about Alfred, and a tear escaped his eye. He tried reading one of his second-hand books, but the story's words couldn't capture his interest. A sound came from the road, then it stopped. A few moments later, a loud pounding on his door scared Bill. He didn't check his peephole because of the cold; he had stuffed it with a cloth for the winter. He picked up a shovel he kept inside to clean off his porch and trails and yelled, "Who's there?"

"The two wise men," Alfred answered; Bert giggled.

"The two wise what?"

As he opened the door, Bill questioned, "Boys, what are you doing here?"

"Spending an early Christmas with you," Al said as he helped Bert place the boxes on the table. The old man was in disbelief and had trouble taking it all in.

"My word, you sure know how to cheer an old man up." Bill proclaimed, holding back tears.

Alfred turned and saw the bunk bed, "What is this?"

"It's a place for Bert to sleep when you guys can stay for a while." Bill proposed.

"Did you build this yourself, Mr. Dennis?" Bert questioned as he looked it over."

"I sure did with God's help," Bill responded.

"Wow, I can't believe you would build this just for me," Bert asserted.

"Man, what a great job." Alf commended.

The boys sat on the couch and still had headroom. Bill told the boys to make themselves comfy. Alfred filled Bill in on all the news since they were there in July.

The boys began to unpack the Christmas tree and flicked on the colorful mini lights. They put the gifts around the little tree on the table and asked Bill, "How does it look?"

"It's a grand sight. Since your mom was little, I haven't had a Christmas tree, Alfred. We lived in that old house then. I'll show you what's left of the old place someday. My cabin needed this Christmas tree, and I'll enjoy it for years to come."

Bill added, "I have something for you, Alfred; I got it from Mr. Taylor, who owns the campground. I was going to surprise you when you came to stay, but now you will have something to look forward to when you come to live here. It will give you some freedom to go places. I feel bad that I don't have something to give you, Bert; I didn't know I'd have Christmas guests," Bill conveyed.

"No problem, Mr. Dennis; we didn't come out here to get presents; we came to give presents and spend time with you," Bert said with a warm smile.

"Thanks for understanding, Bert. Come to the shed, and I'll show you what I've got for you, Alfie, Bill coached.

They walked outside through a few inches of snow to get to the shed. Bill unlocked the shed and opened the door. Bill had the bike standing up front on its kickstand. He had washed and polished it, and it looked almost new.

"Wow! I can't believe this; it's beautiful and a mountain bike too." Alfie turned and hugged the old man tightly and said, "Thank you very much."

"Come on, boys, let's get back inside where it's warm," Bill suggested.

They stomped around the porch to get the snow off before entering. Al and Bert removed their coats, hung them behind the door, and sat on the couch.

"Well, boys, do you want to hear a story?" Old Bill asked.

"Sure," encouraged Bert while Alf nodded in agreement.

"Close your eyes and try to picture the story in your mind," Bill told them to relax.

He picked up a small bottle of Frankincense and Myrrh oil he had bought at Jacks Snacks.

"Nice and relaxed?" Bill questioned; the boys nodded.

"Shepherds sat watching their sheep at night when suddenly a bright light appeared. The light came from the radiance of God's glory and surrounded an angel. The men were terrified, but the angel reassured them, "Do not be afraid. I bring you good news that will cause great joy for all people. Today in the town of David, a Savior has been born to you; he is the Messiah, the Lord."

A great crowd of heavenly beings appeared with the angel and began singing praises to God, "Glory to God in the highest heaven, and peace on earth."

As the angelic beings departed, the shepherds said, "Let's go to Bethlehem and see the Christ-child!" They hurried to the village and found Mary, Joseph, and baby Jesus. They bowed themselves. When they left, they told everyone what the angel said about the newborn Messiah, then they went on their way, praising God.

Later, wise men from the east came to see Jesus. They had followed a big, bright star for many miles, knowing the star signified the birth of the king of the Jews. They continued until they found the newborn king and his mother in Bethlehem.

The wise men bowed and worshiped him, offering treasures of gold, frankincense, and myrrh," Bill paused, opened the tiny essential oil bottle, and dropped a drop on the stove. Soon the aroma of frankincense and myrrh filled the cabin.

Imagine, boys. God loves his human creation so much that he sent his only Son to be born a man through a virgin birth. Jesus experienced life on earth as humans do. He had compassion for people, healed them, and taught them a better way to live by following His example and God's commandments. I don't know if December twenty-fifth is the exact day of the Lord's birth; however, we can celebrate His birthday and be thankful every day of the year that He came to save us.

"You can open your eyes now. I thought it was fitting to tell the Christmas story, and I hope you enjoyed it as much as I did," Bill concluded.

"Bert piped up and said, "Thank you, Mr. Dennis, you have a way of bringing the story to life for me."

Bill expressed, "You guys have made me very grateful and happy."

"We loved doing this for and with you," Al confirmed, smiling.

"Okay," Bill said, rubbing his hands together in anticipation of opening the presents. Alf got up and handed him the first present. Bill's gifts thrilled him. His eyes sparkled as he carefully removed the wrapping without ripping the paper.

"Look at all these goodies; cookies, Nanaimo bars, pecan tarts, shortbread, and Christmas cake," Bill remarked, then confessed, "I'm glad I like to wear baggy pants so I can hide all the weight I'm going to gain; please thank your dear mom for all of this, Bert."

Al and Bert handed Bill the last two gifts that contained the clothing.

"How did you know I needed socks? I love this sweater, too; these should keep me toasty warm. Thank you, boys, you've made me so happy." he said warmly.

"We thought you could always use a sweater and an extra pair of socks," Alfred said.

The rest of the day went by, and since they hadn't planned to stay, they had to go home.

Old Bill sadly waved goodbye and shouted, "Thank you again, and Merry Christmas!"

CHAPTER FOURTEEN

Sabean Survived the Winter

Psalm 50:10-11 ESV

For every beast of the forest is mine,
the cattle on a thousand hills.

I know all the birds of the hills and
all that moves in the field.

Winter passed, and Sabean's wolf background was evident. The wolfdog was a little on the lean side but still quite muscular. Since the first night of her abandonment, Sabean always made her home under that same evergreen. She often went hungry throughout the winter, which improved her hunting skills.

Sabean awoke to a familiar smell she had smelt at her old home a few times; bacon called her, and she followed. She walked a different path to find the source of the delicious aroma. Finally, she came across a cabin. Fearful, Sabean hid in the bushes when suddenly the cabin door opened; a man came out. He wore a camouflage jacket and matching ball cap. The old man sat on a rocker in front of the cabin with a cup of tea. He hummed a little tune to himself as he embraced the splendor of nature. After he finished his tea, Bill stood up and entered his cabin. He kept the door open when making breakfast because he found it too warm in his cabin now that Spring was approaching. Sabean watched him for a long time. She started feeling slightly more relaxed. Bill came out again and descended the stairs, so Sabean thought it was time to go.

It was now the end of March, and Sabean's instincts had become more wolf than dog. She spotted a gopher and ran fast yet quietly and caught herself breakfast. As much as she enjoyed her catch, her attention returned to the pleasant smell of bacon; it brought back the memory of Michael and the smell of cooking from the trailer. She often got a slice of something tasty from Michael before he went to school. Her favorite slice was bacon. Sabean's eyes had a far-off look as she returned to her tree and lay back down. The fur around her neck from the chain that used to imprison her had grown back beautifully. Sabean's spring coat was starting to come through. Feeling satisfied with her morning breakfast, she had a nap.

The next day she made her way to Bill's cabin again. The food smelt so good on this cool morning. It wasn't long before the man came out with his tea; as he sat, he could see Sabean among the bushes. Bill wasn't sure if the animal was a dog or a wolf. He knew it was all by itself. Bill went inside and brought out a plate with some bannock; it had been soaking in yesterday's stew. Sabean observed as the man returned with the plate, and the smell made Sabean drool. The old man walked down the steps a few meters out in the yard and placed the dish down. Sabean could smell the stew that saturated the bannock. She also got a scent of Patchouli oil. Sizing the man up, she recognized the camouflage hat. The man walked up the stairs and returned to his rocker on the porch. Sabean wanted to devour the tantalizing treat but hesitated due to fear of man. However, the familiar smell of Patchouli oil seemed to relax her a bit. After sitting outside for a while, Bill went back into the cabin. Sabean saw her chance, ran to the bannock, and consumed it quickly. She finished the last piece and then noticed the man and the ball cap he wore standing on the porch. The cap made Sabean miss Michael, but she ran back into the bush, still cautious.

She traveled down to the lake and took some licks of water. She felt restless and had difficulty settling down lately.

She was very familiar with her area, and so far, she hadn't had any problems with the other wildlife except for some noisy crows. Although a bit thin, Sabean is a magnificent-looking animal in good health. Her build was that of a small wolf, and her teeth gleamed sharp and dangerous. She could hear her relative's howl in the far distance; she returned the call.

The need to belong somewhere was complex; accepted into an established pack is dangerous for any wolf, more or less a half-wolf. Sabean returned to her burrow and rested her head on her paws; the night closed in as she slept.

The ground still had some snow and ice on it. The morning sun shone brightly, melting the top layer of snow on the hills. Sabean's stomach rumbled when she woke up, so she trotted off to find food. Sabean sniffed the air; following her nose, she lapped up some freshwater near the edge of Spirit Lake. Something was moving in the lake; the animal walked into the lake and found small fish darting back and forth. Staring at the fish for a while, she finally leaped into the water onto what she thought was a fish. Sabean repeated this performance until she finally caught one and walked back onto the beach.

As another day ended, she encountered a couple of rabbits, but they were seasoned and educated in getting away. Then something caught her nose; sniffing the air, she determined the smell was coming from the east. Following her nose, she ventured through the bush until she came upon Bill's cabin.

Bill was whistling to himself as he stirred a pot of soup. The smell drifted outside his window. Sabean, as if hypnotized, slowly walked up to the cabin.

"Well, now, it's you again," said Bill through the opened window. He wasn't used to animals near his door, so seeing this animal sniffing near his steps surprised him. He removed his cap and scratched his head.

Sabean was still cautious, but her tail wagged as the old fellow began to talk to her. Bill opened the door and approached her, but Sabean ran away. He went back inside and continued to stir his soup. Looking back outside, he saw Sabean peeking through the bush.

He said in a loud voice, "I have plenty of soup if you want a bit, but you must trust me. Come and get it."

Sabean watched as Bill came onto his wooden porch and sat in the rocker.

"Mm, sure is good; too bad you're such a skittery thing," Bill said, smiling.

The smell of food was too much for Sabean. She slowly walked out of the bush and ventured near the cabin again. Bill went inside, took out a bowl, filled it with soup, walked out, down the steps, and laid the bowl on the lawn near the cabin steps.

He said, "Okay, here's a bit for you." He turned and walked up the stairs, and sat down.

Sabean licked her lips and began to walk toward the bowl. It might have been the patchouli-smelling cap, and jacket Bill wore that quieted her heart because the man seemed to strike Sabean as someone she could trust.

Bill walked down the steps to retrieve the bowl. Sabean stepped back and moved a few meters away. A few minutes later, Bill returned with another bowl of soup.

"Come on now. I'm not going to hurt you." Old Bill cooed as he placed the soup on the bottom step.

Carefully, Sabean approached the porch step; she stared at the man expecting him to get up and hurt her. The wolfdog took one step, then another, till her mouth reached the bowl. She licked it up like a vacuum cleaner and retreated across the yard.

"Now that is fast, my goodness, you are hungry. I guess I can give you a little bit more." Bill quietly said as he slowly stood up and retrieved the bowl. As he reached down to pick up the bowl, Sabean took off.

Bill went back into the cabin and filled another bowl. Looking out his door, he could see Sabean peeking out of the bushes again. The old bloke went outside and placed the bowl on the middle stair.

It wasn't long before the animal came out of the bush, ran over, and gulped up the soup on the stair. It seemed Sabean took her time eating, and when done, she stepped back down, walked a few paces to a tree, and sat down. She licked her paws and observed Bill sitting on his rocker, enjoying the last of his soup; Sabean's stomach felt full. Sabean wandered off through the brush, seeing there was no more food. Finding a hedge of pussy willows, she laid down beside them. She felt so contented she put her head down and went to sleep. After a short nap, Sabean ran down to the lake. The freshwater tasted good. Some Canadian geese flew above, returning to the area. Their honks were loud, and soon they flew down to the other side of the lake. The sky became dark as the day wore on, and the wind blew hard. Sabean decided it might be time to go to her burrow; once there, the half-wolf snuggled away from the elements.

Sabean awoke to geese honking in the distance. She headed to the lake and tried to run after some of the geese that had landed nearby. She soon found out this was not a good idea. The wolfdog pranced aggressively toward the geese only to have them turn with lifted wings, loudly hissing and honking as they began to chase her. She stopped, not understanding why these prey were not running away. She continued toward them slowly. Suddenly, some geese flew up right in front of her, which scared her. The other geese began quickly waddling after her, displaying their grey and white wings. Confused, she turned and ran away. Sabean sped off into the bush until she could hardly hear the menacing honks.

Early the following day, there was a smell of something in the air, and it smelt good. Sabean followed her nose to the old man's cabin. Feeling more relaxed, she sat in the clearing near the cabin. She saw the man enjoying his breakfast of bannock, eggs, and tea.

Sabean focused on Bill's camouflage cap, and again she was reminded of the one Michael wore. She stared at him until the man felt her eyes on him and looked up.

"Oh, you're back, and I bet you're hungry. I have no soup left, but I'll let you lick my plate when I finish.

Sabean stared at Bill until she saw him put his plate on the porch's top step. There were some leftover eggs and a bit of bannock on it. Sabean moved to the porch, climbed the stairs, and devoured the leftovers. After she finished, she stepped back and stared at Bill again.

"I suppose you want more bannock now," Bill assumed as he went inside and brought out a piece. He walked out, put the plate on the porch near his rocker, and sat down.

"Well, here you go, but you must come and get it," Bill said.

Before feeling safe enough to venture close to the man, Sabean looked at the food for quite a while; she ran up the stairs, took the bannock in her mouth, and trotted off happily to the bush line, where she sat down and enjoyed the food. Sabean started to feel more comfortable with the man wearing the camouflage ball cap. As time passed, she often came for food, and by the end of the third week, she took her morning bannock from Bill's hand.

One morning Bill sat, enjoying the outdoors, deep in thought. He closed his eyes and fell asleep. Upon waking, he noticed something beside him, lying on the porch; it was Sabean.

"How long have you been here, girl? Bill asked. He leaned down and petted the top of the animal's head. Sabean's tail wagged, then she stood up, wanting more attention. The old fellow rubbed her sides, then her ears. She loved this attention and became entirely trusting of him.

"You are a beautiful girl," Bill said while petting the animal.

Bill and Sabean had become friends. He knew she had to have wolf in her by how she walked. Knowing wolves, Bill knew quite a bit about them and knew to let the wolf come to him rather than invade her immediate space. Knowing these things helped Sabean trust him. It wasn't long before Bill would get her to come to him; he would pat the side of his leg, and she would run over. Life was better for both of them.

Sabean laid back down. Bill sat with a wide satisfying smile at the thought that he had made friends with the part wolf. His grin broadened as he thought of his grandson coming to live with him when he finished school. It would be great if the animal accepted Alfie, Bill thought. The old fellow wasn't sure why Sabean took to him, but he was glad she did. He adjusted his cap, then dozed off.

CHAPTER FIFTEEN

Paul Gives In To Temptation

Paul had been thinking about the great times he had spent with his old buddies by the lake in summers past, but he had no friends now. He could feel the enemy tempting him, trying to lure him back to his old life. Paul became very depressed. Instead of praying to the Lord for help, Paul felt the only help he needed was reaching out to his friends. He realized that due to some chemical imbalance or something in his body, he mustn't drink alcohol.

The thoughts in Paul's life put him in a bad mood most of the time. Just about anything would tick him off. He felt his buddies had abandoned him. He was lonely for his friends. His need for alcohol and friends became more vital, and Paul felt he couldn't take it much longer.

One night Paul got himself so worked up that he shook his fist high at the ceiling and yelled at God, "Leave me alone; I can't take it anymore: God, stop picking on me." Paul shouted, *and the devil laughed.*

Joyce shouted that Satan was tempting him, but Paul didn't listen. Paul continued swearing at God with his vulgar mouth while thrusting his fist up at Him.

Things were up and down in the Ross home for a while. At least Paul tried not to take his frustrations out on his family. He was aware the police knew he used to push Joyce around. Officer Lehman said he'd be watching him.

Bernie's last words to him were, "If I hear of any problems at home, Paul, you can expect another visit to the jail for a very long time."

That night Paul sat in his chair, not saying a word. Hours went by without any conversation.

Joyce finally said that if Paul wanted to meet new friends, he should consider attending church with her and Mike.

"You know I don't like most people at the church, and they don't like me. I don't like having to sing either." Paul informed.

"Why not at least try and get to know some people there? You may meet someone who likes to fish and hunt." Joyce suggested.

"End of subject!" Paul shouted.

The phone rang, and it was Pastor Josh. Paul answered, and his face displayed annoyance. Paul claimed he was too busy to have him over and would call him when he was free.

Joyce thought that Paul wasn't even trying to help himself. Paul sat in silence for the rest of the evening.

The next night Paul called Brian to see how he was doing. Brian asked if he would like to get out for a while.

Paul said, "Sure, Brian, but I can't drink liquor."

"Still?" Brian asked.

"Doctor's orders," Paul responded.

"Okay, but you can still keep me company." Brian reasoned, then said, "I'll be there soon."

Paul put his arms around Joyce and said, "Brian is picking me up, but don't worry, I will be drinking pop." Paul kissed Joyce, smiled, and told her she was beautiful.

The bar was jumping, but Paul was sober and bored. He looked around and saw all the action and missed it. His fourth fountain drink tasted sugary sweet in his mouth, and Paul couldn't drink another. He thought one beer wouldn't hurt me? He could feel himself weakening but tried to hang on without success.

Brian said, "I wonder how you got mixed with religion."

"I didn't. I accepted Jesus as my Saviour, but I don't go to church or anything." Paul announced.

"Oh, I see," Brian said.

Brian used to go to church a few years ago and knew some scriptures. He looked at Paul and said, "God will forgive you of your sins, so why not just have one beer?"

His friends were thrilled when they heard Paul order a beer. The beer went down like silk, so he ordered another. By the end of the evening, Paul had trouble negotiating his way to Brian's van and almost fell. Brian was also drunk but started his van and drove Paul home without incident.

When Paul crawled into bed, Joyce pretended to be asleep, but she could smell the liquor. It wasn't long before she heard her husband snoring. Paul hadn't been drinking since he got out of prison, so Joyce hoped this was a one-off. As she lay awake, she thought about some of the changes she had seen in him lately. Joyce wondered if Paul would start drinking every day again.

Morning came, and Joy awoke alone. Paul had got up and left without saying goodbye.

Paul spent most of his free time with Brian and the boys, and Joyce and Michael missed him.

They had enjoyed the weekly board games where the three played together and laughed. They also missed just being together and watching comedy on TV.

Paul didn't even seem to want to talk about Christ anymore. The liquor had let out the demons in Paul's mind.

Joyce thought, is my nightmare about to begin again?

She had a nice supper waiting for Paul when he got home that night. Paul walked home, opened the door, threw his coat on the floor, and looked at Joyce.

Paul grumbled, "It will cost an arm and a leg to fix my truck, so I'll have to cut down on the grocery money. Speaking of groceries, when is dinner ready?"

"It's ready now," Joyce replied.

Paul sat at the supper table. Michael came in and said hello to his dad. Paul grunted, "Hi,"

Joyce placed the food on the table. Mike started to tell his parents about his day when Paul pounded the table and told him to shut up and eat.

Paul said, "I don't want to hear about your dribble."

Joyce took offense and said, "You don't have to be like that, Paul."

Paul leaned over and informed her that he was the head of the house, then shouted,

"If I want quiet, then it better be quiet, and I don't need any lip from you, either, lady."

Paul finished his meal, went into the living room, turned on the TV, and tuned it to the Sports channel. Joyce and Michael looked perplexed at Paul's return to his old ways.

It was another cold February day. No matter how Joy tried not to think about the situation with Paul, the sadness in her heart finally took its toll. Joyce placed her hands under her chin and sat at the kitchen table; she felt discouraged.

Paul knew he would go back to jail if he abused his family again, so Paul spent his time mainly with his friends. When he was home, he watched TV silently. Hours of silence, night after night, depressed Joyce. Rather than sit in the living room with Paul, she felt strangely less alone sitting in the kitchen by herself.

Joyce raised her head and looked solemnly out the window. She bowed her head and prayed.

"Dear Jesus, will I ever be happy again?" She asked between tears.

CHAPTER SIXTEEN

Alfred Goes to Live With His Granddad

Today was report card day at Canby School, and Alfred was apprehensive about how the day would turn out. He got dressed and went downstairs. His mother was still asleep in her bedroom. Alf felt a weight lift off his shoulders when he saw his mother wasn't around to scream threats at him if he failed grade nine again.

Alfie had gathered his few belongings and put them in his pillowcase with PJs, underwear, and a toothbrush; he put it under his pillow and covered it with his blanket, knowing he'd be leaving after school. Alfred grabbed a big flashlight that no one ever seemed to use. He thought the flashlight would be handy at the cabin, including finding his way to the outhouse at night. Al tucked the bag under his pillow; he was ready for a quick exit.

Larry thinking only of himself, grabbed two of the three pizza pieces left from dinner the night before as he left for school. Finding only one piece of pizza, Al put it in a bag and saved it for later. He was hungry in the morning but was used to ignoring his stomach growls, knowing he would have something to eat later. Alfie thought he shouldn't be surprised because it wasn't the first day he had gone without food; at least he had that one piece of pizza.

Arriving at school, he endured the usual dirty names and laughter. Head down, Alfred made his way to the side of the school.

He saw something from the corner of his eye. It was Bert who waved and called him over. Al made his way to Bert.

With seriousness written on his face, Bert said, "This is the big day, Alf. I hope you pass."

Al looked Bert in the eyes and said, "I am not looking forward to it, but I have a plan.

"A plan, what kind of plan, Alfred?" Bert questioned.

"I'm going to share something with you, and you can't tell anyone, okay," Al said.

"Okay, you know you can trust me; what is it?" Bert asked.

"You know I don't have a very nice home life, and my family has never wanted me around. To prove this, if I fail again this year, mom said she'd kick me out of the house permanently," Alf shared.

"My friend, what are you going to do?" Bert asked with concern in his voice.

"Granddad told me if mom kicks me out, I could go and live with him," Al said as a smile spread across his face.

"Wow, I thought I heard your granddad say something about you moving in. I didn't think it would be so soon. Alfred, I will miss you so much," Bert said sadly.

"I hope you'll come out often to see us because I will miss you too. Remember, you have a bed there now," Al said.

"You can count on me, buddy. I'll be out as much as possible; I could help you with some chores and pick some supplies you might need if you phone me from the campground phone." Bert offered.

The school bell rang, so they went to their classrooms.

Loud voices and laughter filled the halls of the school. Some were looking forward to the summer holidays, and some were looking forward to their report card results.

"All right now, settle down," Mr. Dixon said at the top of his voice.

The class became quiet. Mr. Dixon went over what they could expect on this last school day. Finally, the lunch bell rang, and the school halls became very loud again. They knew they would receive their report cards after lunch, and then they could leave for the summer ahead.

Alfred realized he would probably never see Mrs. Forbes again, which saddened him. She was so good to him and always encouraged him.

He returned to the school and found Mrs. Forbes. Al asked if he could talk to her.

Sandra said, "Let's go into the library."

They sat down together, and Al's eyes filled with tears. The young man wiped his eyes. Sandra asked what the problem was. Alfred regained his composure and thanked her for all she had done for him.

"You were the only teacher who tried to help me, and I am good at math because of you, Mrs. Forbes. My mom will kick me out if I fail again, and we both know I have." Al confided.

"What are you going to do, Alfred?" she asked.

"Don't worry about me, Mrs. Forbes, because I've got a plan, and to be honest, I am looking forward to it," Alf said confidently.

"I will miss you, Alfred, and I'll keep you in my prayers," Sandra said as tears rose.

The bell rang. Al thanked her again and then made his way to his homeroom. Mr. Dixon handed out the reports, and many kids smiled at their results. Before opening it, Alfred sat with the report closed on his desk for quite some time.

Al drew a deep breath and then let it out as he opened his report card. Alfred had indeed failed. He put the report back in its envelope and left for home. Larry and his pals walked up behind Alf and began taunting him.

"You failed again, didn't you frog breath," Larry yelled loudly so all could hear. Al kept walking and tried his best to ignore them.

Larry and his friends gave up on hassling Al and wanted to celebrate their summer holidays at the Janice café. Al walked into his home to his mother and dad's angry faces.

"Well, let's see it," Darlene demanded. Al handed her the envelope and prepared himself for the worse. Preparation was wise because he could feel the overbearing tension rise in the room. Al sat on the couch, his eyes closed, waiting for the blow. Darlene threw the report on the floor and then began to beat Al with an empty wine bottle until it broke on his back. Darlene's face was pure evil as she held on to the broken neck of the bottle. She threw it at him but missed. Al knew it was coming and managed to avert it. Darlene picked up the broken bottle again and came next to his face.

"Get out of my house and never return, you useless fool. I just want you out of my life so I can forget I ever had you," Darlene said with commitment. Still holding the broken bottle, she warned him to get going before she did something terrible. Alfred teared up to find out just how much his mother hated him. His father just stood there saying nothing.

Al's face was red. He ran upstairs, retrieved his bag under the pillow, slipped it under his jacket, and ran down the stairs. He opened the door without saying a word and left. Al didn't look back as he shut the door behind him.

He bought some batteries for the flashlight, then went out to the highway and stuck out his thumb as he walked backward. Surprisingly enough, it wasn't long before someone stopped and picked him up. The driver's name was Hank, and he was a talker. They talked about his experiences and much more until Al told him he was a Christian.

"Oh, come on, kid, don't tell me you're mixed up in that malarky. When you die, that is it.

No heaven, no hell," Hank said.

"My grandfather could tell you things about Jesus that would change your mind." Al countered.

Hank looked annoyed and stopped talking. He drove Alfred to where the gravel road started, near the campground sign. Alf thanked him with a smile. Hank looked at Al, then looked ahead and drove off.

Alfred arrived around 4 p.m. As he made his way to the cabin, he realized how happy he was. Alf knocked on the door and heard movement inside. Not expecting company

Bill looked through the peephole and opened the door. His heart filled with joy to see his grandson had finally arrived.

"Wow, I didn't expect you, boy. Come in and sit down and tell me what is going on," Bill said with a smile.

"You meant it when you said I could come and live with you? Alfred asked.

Old Bill nodded and said, "Are you here with me for good because you are a most welcomed sight to these old eyes of mine?"

"Oh, I am so happy to be here, and it feels good that you honestly want me. Mom has kicked me out," He paused, then continued, "I failed school again," Alfie said with a sheepish look.

"My dear boy, my home is your home." Old Bill said as he hugged Alfred tightly, then continued, "I'm going to teach you how to live out here, and there is a lot to learn, so I hope you're up for it."

Alfred's face shone with excitement, and he said, "I can't wait, and I feel I belong for the first time in my life,"

"You do belong here. You are loved and will be a big help to me," Bill admitted.

He asked if Al was hungry, and the boy nodded. Bill brought down a couple of bowls, filled them with hot soup, and took some bannock out from a pan.

"Wow, this is good soup, but I don't think I have ever tasted anything like it," the young man said.

Bill smiled and said, "It's what I call God's herb soup, and depending on what type of herbs I put in dictates how it will taste."

They talked and took their time eating dinner. After dinner, Alfred grabbed his bag, pulled out the big flashlight, and said, "Look what I have for us; it's been sitting in the junk drawer for years, and nobody ever uses it, so I bought new batteries, and it works great." Al said.

"Wow, look how bright it is," the old guy said gleefully. "Thank you, Al, this will really come in handy," Bill said, looking over the flashlight.

"Feel like a game of checkers?" Bill asked.

"Sure do," Al said. After a few games, Alf and Bill started to yawn, so Bill suggested they go to bed.

Alf woke to the sound of birds and the smell of pancakes. He rubbed his eyes and sat up. Bill was already up, dressed, and making pancakes right on the stove. The stove had to be about as old as Bill is. It had a large cooking area with a metal plate attached, which made an excellent warming shelf where Bill put the fresh pancakes. He turned and saw the boy was awake.

"Come on, boy, time to get up; breakfast is ready, and I have plans for us today," Bill said.

After many pancakes, the two sat for a bit, and Bill suggested they clean up the dishes and go for a walk. Al volunteered to wash up the dishes and then sweep the floor. Bill went outside and returned with two buckets.

"Grab a bucket for our walk; we can pick plants," Bill announced.

It was a beautiful day, and the country's smells were refreshing as they went on their morning stroll. The dew was still on the ground; the mornings in the Alberta bush were full of life. The sun shone, making sparkling spider webs decorations among bush branches.

"See these wild roses? Bill asked. They'll produce rose hips, and we'll pick every good one in the fall. They make a tasty tea, and a guy should drink many cups of it in the winter to ward off colds."

"Look here, Alfie," Bill said, pointing to a weed called Lamb's Quarters, "We'll boil the leaves and mix them with garlic, onions, and bacon fat; now that's good eating. It is also a way to get Vitamin C." Bill picked some Horsetail and explained its qualities as they walked,

"We'll dry this out for tea. It's good for the heart and lungs, plus a good tonic when you're run-down."

They came upon a wet area where wild mint grew. Bill told Alfie to collect the leaves. Bill explained he likes to have lots of mint on hand because it is a great way to drink some of the teas he makes. It hides some plants' awful taste, and picking mint encourages new growth.

"You will never be bored here, my boy. I am glad I don't have to do it all by myself anymore," Bill said, smiling.

Bill warned, "As autumn sets in, we'll spend some time in the cabin with wall-to-wall screening trays filled with herbs to dry; it will smell very woodsy in there. We will have to check the traps twice a day when winter comes, no matter how cold it gets. I wouldn't want my catch to freeze; we'll just bundle up. I find the cold air slaps me across the face when I first head outside at that time of the year."

Bill placed food in the catch cage, set up the trap door, and strategically placed the traps. Bill never used leg-hold traps as he felt it was a cruel way to catch his dinner. If he caught a rabbit, the animal wouldn't freeze to death because Bill's kill is always quick and humane; he respects all animals.

They walked over to the campground after checking the traps. Alfred thought to himself how refreshing Spirit Lake would be this summer.

Bill said, "Of course, there are not many ready to camp yet, but it won't be long. Good fishing in the lake brings them here too," the old man added, "Do you know how to fish, Alfred?"

"I've never fished before, but I'm sure you'll teach me. Al responded.

Alfie looked at the small campground cabins and found them well-built but not cozy like their cabin.

"Granddad, the man that gave me a ride up claimed Christianity and the Gospel are just stories made up by man, and Jesus is just a crutch to lean on, and the man believes that when we die, that's the end. No heaven and no hell."

"I believe that man is in for a big surprise," Bill commented, "Just for a moment, let's say he's right, and if so, he'll have nothing to fear, but my dear boy, what will that person do when he finds out that the Gospel of Jesus Christ is true and we were right? It will be too late then."

They filled their pails, "Let's head back, Al," Bill said as they walked through the bush onto a narrow path.

Bill saw Sabean lying on the lawn beside the cabin steps as they returned. Bill stopped abruptly and said quietly, "Stop and be very quiet; there's someone I want you to meet."

Alfred saw the animal and followed Bill's instructions. Bill slowly walked over to Sabean and gently said, "Good morning, girl; there is someone I want you to meet."

Sabean spotted Alfred, stood up, and ran off.

"Who's that?" Al asked with surprise in his voice.

"That's my friend," Bill explained, then continued, "I'm not sure where she's from, but I know she's part wolf. She was probably abandoned, or she may have run away. The number of dogs people drop off in the bush to fend for themselves is sad just because they are not wanted anymore."

"So, she trusts you?" Alfie asked.

"It took a while, but yes, we have become good friends, but I warn you, don't approach her without me for a while, but I'm sure she'll come around," Bill encouraged.

It took a couple of weeks, but sure enough, the half-wolf learned to trust Alfred and would walk up to him, expecting to be either petted or fed. Sabean still slept in her burrow at night but often showed up in front of the cabin during the day, mooching for scraps; she was never disappointed.

CHAPTER SEVENTEEN

Tembah Leaves the Rocky Hill Pack

Psalm 145:15-16 ESV

*All eyes look to you, and you give
them their food in due season.*

*You open your hand; you satisfy the
desire of every living thing.*

The pack returned from a night of hunting dragging an old deer. They had gorged themselves on the beast. Wolves are known to eat several pounds of meat in one sitting; they know each meal could be their last and fill up as much as possible.

Tembah, now sixteen months old, had been pushing his weight around. Today was no exception because he got too close to Growler for comfort. Growler turned on him. Tembah didn't back down. They fought for a few minutes until Tembah, knowing he wasn't a match for Growler, turned and ran away.

Tembah lay behind a tree licking his wounds. He wanted to be free from the restrictions he encountered in the pack.

Tembah knew he didn't belong, and after he felt better, he decided it was time to leave and strike out on his own;

It is not unusual for male wolves to leave the pack to find a mate and start a new pack.

After running for some time, Tembah sat down to rest. It wasn't long before he could hear the pack's howls become louder, and he knew he must move on. Tembah was now a lone wolf and not part of the pack anymore; The black wolf knew he would be a forgotten member of the Rocky Hill Pack. He ran and walked the rest of the day and into the night until he could hardly move anymore. Tembah was tired and hungry.

A few days passed, and the young wolf could barely hear his old pack the further west he went. He had covered several miles southwest of where he started. He stopped and looked for a place to rest, and as he settled down, he heard something moving in the high grass. It was a big fat marmot. Although exhausted, his stomach ordered him to give chase. Tembah ran with all his might and was able to grab the meal; he lay down, and the food soothed his aching stomach.

The sun began showing itself as the young wolf finally fell asleep. He dreamed about the pack. Tembah's body and eyes twitched as he moved about in his dream. He dreamt that his mother was in trouble and woke up whimpering.

Tembah found it hard to find prey he could handle without the pack, but he became quite proficient as a lone wolf as time passed. That night Tembah came upon a half-eaten deer. He dove into the meat without looking around first; he was hungry. A growling pack of coyotes didn't like him helping himself to their prey and began to surround him. Tembah backed away from the fallen animal, then turned and ran. A pack of coyotes can easily kill a lone wolf. They ran after him but soon gave up the chase and returned to their kill.

Finally, feeling safe, Tembah found some shade and lay down. He rested, then moved again further west. He found a small cave that sheltered him throughout the winter ahead. The wolf was lonely but managed somehow.

Tembah's loneliness became more prevalent as time passed, so he left his shelter one day. He traveled all night until daybreak. He stopped by Spirit Lake and lapped up the cold, refreshing water. Feeling tired, he found a spot to lie down. He hadn't slept very long when he awoke to noises from the bush. It was a large rabbit. Tembah, now a seasoned lone hunter, took no time running the animal down. After a scuffle, he enjoyed his dinner just as the sun rose.

The big black wolf was getting increasingly aggressive now that spring approached. His male instinctual urges were becoming more potent; he needed a mate.

The sun's warmth felt good on his body. He smelt something quite enticing. He felt his body becoming excited. Carefully he walked around some tall Poplar trees. Tembah came to a clearing and saw the most exciting sight of his life. It was Sabean. She was cleaning herself under a tree in front of a cabin. After a thorough cleaning, she began to head back to her den.

Careful to be quiet, Tembah followed her. He could smell man, which made his guard hair stand on end. Reaching her burrow under the evergreen, Sabean lay down and didn't come out for some time. The wolf found a place nearby to watch her. Tembah was mesmerized by Sabean.

The black wolf watched her from his hiding place. The sight of Sabean was almost too much for him to resist; still, he remained in the bushes.

Sabean spent most of the next day at Bill's, eating and sleeping, but as evening came, she left. As she walked through familiar animal trails, she smelt something new that attracted and frightened her simultaneously. Sabean could see something in the trees and then spotted the wolf.

Tembah approached her very carefully so as not to spook her. He saw she wasn't quite as large as Tembah's sisters but female. Unable to resist her any longer, he walked toward her. He saw she was a beautiful wolf cross. Scared and growling, Sabean made it known she wouldn't be easy to get to know. Tembah stopped in his tracks and just stood and stared at her. The wolfdog turned and ran. The big male followed her at a distance but was determined to make her his mate. Sabean ran away but eventually circled back under her evergreen tree. She was strangely attracted to that black wolf. After staring at him through the tree's boughs, she finally had enough nerve to make her way out from under the tree by morning.

The morning air was crisp, and the sun shone brightly. Tembah had hunted that night but only caught frustration. Upon his return, he found Sabean beside her tree.

All at once, the wolf was distracted by a sound in the bush. Tembah's ears pointed straight up as he took off at lightning speed. Sabean followed him to the tantalizing smell of fresh kill. There, still gorging himself, was a black bear. The young wolf remained patient, out of sight, and downwind from the bear. Sabean silently came closer but stayed behind some brush. The bear had finally eaten his fill and slowly waddled away.

When Tembah felt safe, he walked over to the remains and began to eat. Sabean crouched down with her tail between her legs in submission to the wolf, then moved cautiously toward him. He snarled at her at first but soon gave way, allowing her to fill her hungry stomach. With stomachs full, they moved on from the downed animal. Their eyes met, still somewhat distrusting each other; Sabean tightened as Tembah slowly moved closer. He walked up to Sabean, and she let him lick her face. There was an exchange of licking, and then they slowly walked back to Sabean's burrow under the tree. They were weary; they lay tightly next to each other. Howls from the Rocky Hill Pack rang out in the far distance. Tembah stood up and returned the call. Sabean was excited by his response and joined in with a full-fledged howl. After some wolf singing, they lay back down and fell asleep until late afternoon. Tembah stood up, stretched, and walked out from under the tree, as did Sabean.

Tembah held his tail high as he began to dance around playfully. Sabean stared at him, then her tail wagged, and she joined in the play. Tembah stopped, bowed, and raised his rear as if to pounce. They played until they ran out of energy. Sabean walked to her tree den with Tembah at her side. The evening sky displayed itself gloriously as the sun went down.

Tembah woke up. Sabean, already awake, rolled back and forth on her back, then stood up and shook herself. They ran off with their bodies close to each other. After some frolicking and chasing, they sat down. Tembah smelled the air, and his ears twitched back and forth. It wasn't long before they ran off into the forest again. They had accepted one another, and by the end of the evening, they had become devoted mates.

CHAPTER EIGHTEEN

Sabean & Tembah Are Having Pups

Genesis 1:24

And God said, "Let the earth bring forth living creatures according to their kinds—livestock and creeping things and beasts of the earth according to their kinds."

And it was so.

It was a beautiful time of the year in the Alberta Forest. Winds blew through the poplar trees making their leaves sound like they were whispering.

This morning, Sabean started looking for a den to have her pups. She was very particular about where she would spend her time, and nothing pleased her. Finding a suitable spot, the animal worked long and hard on making a nice den while Tembah went off hunting. Upon Tembah's return, She had fashioned herself a cozy den.

Smelling a kill, she whined a bit, then peeked out of her den and trotted down to enjoy Tembah's prey. Once Sabean stomach was full, she returned to her den to make some final touches. She would spend all her time with her pups until they turned three weeks old.

Tembah returned from hunting one morning and could hear the sounds of puppies whimpering inside the den. Sabean had given birth to five healthy pups, four boys and one girl. Teddy, the largest, found his mother's nipples first and was busy filling his tiny stomach. Joe, Copper, Yoda, and the little female Penny quickly joined Teddy and enjoyed their mother's enriched milk feast. Sabean adored her babies and life with Tembah. She still missed Michael and the man at the cabin but hoped to see them again someday.

Winter began to flex its muscles. All was fine in the den, and Tembah was faithful in bringing home enough food to feed his growing family. He was happy with his little pack and became an excellent alpha male. Tembah and Sabean watched their babies grow into beautiful wolves with bodies to match as winter passed. Very little of the domestic dog line showed in the pups.

Penny is the clown of the bunch and loves playing and wrestling with her siblings. Her body and face displayed various brown, cinnamon, and black areas. Her face looked like an angel until she got mad; then, she would portray the tiny terror she was. Joe has an all-white face with light reddish-brown around his ears. His body is primarily white with a touch of brown and gold. Joe was easygoing and liked being with his brother, Copper, who loved playing with him. Copper is a beautiful male and has a wonderful disposition.

Yoda is excitable; any strange noise and his ears would perk up, and his guard hairs stood straight. His whole body was ready for action. Teddy and Yoda were the dominant siblings. Teddy is just a bit larger than Yoda, so when it comes down to a fight, Yoda usually gives in to Teddy and walks away.

The pups were four months old now and full of mischief. They liked to howl with their parents. Although the pups had funny little yelping howls, the family song is eerie, frightening, and somewhat lonesome. It seemed they would make a formable force once the pups grew up.

As winter rolled on, the pups grew to be magnificent wolves; they worked well as a pack when hunting and evolved into a formative and well-synchronized team.

It's hard to believe that Sabean and Tembah were both rejected, but it seemed to fill them with strength and wisdom, which they passed on to their pack.

A herd of elk wandered into their newly formed pack's territory. Tembah smelled them first, then they all became alerted. They ran through an old animal trail single file until the herd came into view. They stopped short and then began to spread out. The herd became aware of the wolves and started to run. Tembah took the lead with Sabean close behind him. The young wolves began chasing the beasts from various directions until they were beside the herd. They ran close but were careful not to get kicked. It took a long time to get in position to attack a deer. Finally, a weak, older female began to falter and fall behind. Closing on the elk, the wolves ascended onto her, pulling her to the ground. Tembah made the kill quick, and soon the animal lay dead. After the wolves were full, they dragged the elk's remains to the pack site. That elk fed the little family for a few days.

Now that the pups were grown, Sabean would go off on her own to visit her old friend Bill. Her visits were short but necessary for her well-being; she was very attached to Bill and never forgot his kindness toward her. Sabean finally accepted Alfred too, which made Al very happy. Sabean's pack would follow her but stay hidden in the bush. Tembah, being all wolf, didn't understand Sabean's fascination with the old guy but seemed to know and accept her rendezvous with the man and his companion. The young wolves did not know any better and accepted that their mother needed these visits. They waited patiently with Tembah until they were all reunited again.

As Sabean left to join her family, Bill saw her pack and her sizeable black mate. Bill was relieved to see she had a pack to keep her safe. He thought to himself the old saying, safety in numbers. The old man didn't get many visits these days, but Sabean returned for a visit when she could.

CHAPTER NINETEEN

The Rocky Hill Pack Grows

Job 12:7-10

*"But ask the animals, and they will teach you, or
the birds in the sky, and they will tell you;*

*or speak to the earth, and it will teach you,
or let the fish in the sea inform you.*

*Which of all these does not know that the
hand of the LORD has done this?*

*In his hand is the life of every creature
and the breath of all mankind.*

Breeze had given birth in late April to four pups, two males and two females; Chance, Jasper, Europia, and Miriah. They were still too young to run with the pack and stayed close to Breeze.

The sun was setting, and the Rocky Hill pack was becoming anxious to hunt. Growler headed southwest because the suckerfish were spawning. The Huckle River would almost appear dark with the number of fish rushing to spawn. The river was about twenty-four km west, and the wolves were anxious to feast on fish while avoiding bears. Duke, Opie, Casey, Rascal, and Lacey were now allowed to run with the older wolves and were ecstatic.

The pack had almost reached their destination when they discovered a half-eaten deer. Bounding up to the carcass wasn't the best of ideas because that deer belonged to a wolverine. Out like a flash came the wolverine, who challenged them by snapping and lunging at them.

Tucker thinking of himself as a mighty fighter, went for the animal and got a vicious bite on his side; he backed away quickly. The wolverine circled the carcass showing aggression and snapping his powerful jaws together at the pack showing its razor-sharp teeth. Growler encountered a wolverine when he was still relatively young; although the pack rescued him, he ended up with a nasty injury to his leg. Growler, now a full-grown adult, never forgot his experienced and indicated to the pack to move on. They left the area and the miserable creature to enjoy his deer. The wind began to blow hard as they approached the Huckle river. Bears occupied the best spots along the river. The pack moved further down the river and began to fish. The young wolves thought this was fun. They jumped around the water with little success in catching a fish. The rest of the pack knew how to fish and soon gorged themselves. After frolicking about in the water, the younger wolves ate the leftovers. Tucker didn't even notice the bite on his side because he was so busy fishing and eating. Filled to the brim, they decided to head back east to their pack site. As they gathered, a black bear started walking in their direction. The wolves wasted no time and ran off. The pack was far enough west to hear howls from Tembah's pack. Growler couldn't resist returning the call, and his pack joined in. They ran east for around two km, then stopped for a rest. Growler was so full he decided to bed down there rather than travel back to their pack site. The young wolves were weary from the trek. The pack slept well this day.

CHAPTER TWENTY

The Last Chapter

The pub was incredibly smoky, and the voices of beer drinkers were loud. Paul sat with Brian and asked if he would be interested in a weekend fishing trip.

"Sorry, buddy, I just can't go, "Brian said, then continued, "The in-laws are in town, and I'm stuck entertaining them."

"Oh man, I just need to get away from this lousy town, but I didn't want to go alone," Paul complained.

"Take the family. That way, you'll have someone to drive and cook the fish," Brian suggested.

"I guess that would work, but it won't be the same as being with you, pal," Paul said.

Paul decided he would call it a night and said goodbye; he staggered a bit as he left the pub, then got into his newly repaired truck. Luckily there were no police around to see him driving and occasionally weaving over the centerline. Paul drove without a license but didn't seem to care. He pulled into his driveway and got out. Paul found Joyce watching TV as he entered and announced they were going camping on the weekend. Joyce was glad that he wanted her and Mike to join him.

"Just the three of us, Paul?" Joyce queried.

"Yeah, so be ready at 5 a.m. sharp Saturday so we can get set up before noon," Paul said with authority.

Saturday came, and the Ross family was in the car and on their road by 5:05 a.m; their destination was the Spirit Lake campground. They arrived at about 5:50 a.m., and Paul told Joyce to set up the camp while he'd go and secure a boat at the dock.

Spirit Lake campground was becoming popular. Tom Taylor, the landowner, had sand hauled in to make a nice beach area and a boat ramp. Four rowboats lay by the beach for rent.

Joyce lugged everything out of the truck to the number eight campsite. Paul didn't want people near him, so he had chosen number eight, the furthest campsite. Mike helped Joyce the best he could, and by 10 a.m., they had everything set up, including the BBQ, a cooler filled with pop and beer, and a table. They set up the tent among the trees with a grassy area in front of it, perfect for chairs. Joyce hauled out the camp chairs, then gathered some twigs and wood for a fire she hoped to enjoy that night.

"Can I go down to the beach, mom?" Mike asked.

"Sure, but stick to the path; we're beside a steep ravine," Joyce pointed to the large warning sign beside the ravine to the right, "So stay to the left side of our tent and follow the trail to the beach," Joyce replied.

Joyce laid back on the lounge chair and finally took it easy. She embraced the sound of the water running swiftly at the bottom of the ravine. Moving her head, she could see the gathering birds, hoping for a handout. Joyce stretched her whole body, then fell back on the lounger and experienced a gentle wind blowing warmly over her; peace for a while, at least.

Paul returned to the camp around 3 p.m. with a couple of fish. He handed them to Joyce to cook for dinner without a word. Paul opened a cold beer from the cooler, then laid down on a lounger.

It was late August, and it seemed only women with children were there, which annoyed Paul. As he sat drinking his beer, he complained that there was no one to talk to, and maybe camping wasn't such a great idea after all. Joyce thought it was too bad Paul didn't consider talking to her. Michael returned with his pail and shovel, and Joyce busied herself cleaning and preparing the fish for dinner.

"Hi, mom; I see we have some fish for dinner.

"Quiet dear, dad is resting," Joyce responded.

"Yea, shut up, kid," Paul grunted back loudly.

"Okay, sorry, can I play down on the beach again? I'll be quiet." Mike said in a low voice as he pointed to the beach.

Joyce said, 'Okay".

It was nearing supper time. Joyce put together a potato salad and then turned on the BBQ.

Paul was resting; his nose twitched as he detected the smell of fish.

Paul stirred himself up, announced he was hungry, and asked if it would be much longer before dinner. Joyce said it was almost ready.

"Come on, Mike, time to get ready for dinner," Joyce shouted, motioning her arm for him to come.

The evening was quiet, and the fire was captivating. The sun was starting to go down, and the Ross family got ready for bed.

Enticed by the smells of the campground, Sabean and her pack checked out the campground and silently surveyed the area. Her nose detected Michael and patchouli oil. Sabean whimpered a bit. Finding nothing to eat, the troop vanished into the night.

The following day Paul didn't try to be quiet when he left. He seemed to enjoy waking everyone up. Paul would always find something to aggravate himself and, as usual, handled it with a barrage of curse words. Paul grabbed his tackle box and the cooler and went down to the rowboat. He was ready for a day of fishing and drinking. Joyce and Mike brushed the sleep from their eyes and crawled out of their sleeping bags.

At noon, Joyce saw Paul come in with a large fish. Paul smiled with pride as he handed his trophy to Joyce. He expressed that the fish he caught deserved an afternoon of beers and relaxation.

Joyce knew that Paul would be drunk and miserable by supper. He is a mean drunk, and Joyce often wondered why he found drinking such a pleasure when it usually brought him anger or depression. By five o'clock, Paul was yelling and cursing at Joyce; Joyce retreated into the tent. Paul fell back to sleep.

Mike had busied himself on the beach for most of the day. He felt like someone was watching him and heard something in the bush. Mike stopped what he was doing and stared in the direction of the noise.

Sabean made her little family wait in the bush. Her heart jumped at the sight of her beloved boy master, and she sprinted over to him. Mike's eyes became huge when he saw Sabean. He opened his arms wide to receive his lost pet.

"Sabean!" Mike yelled at the top of his voice. Sabean wagged her tail in delight.

"I have missed you so much, girl; you have no idea how much I have missed you," Michael said lovingly to his pet while hugging her tightly.

Paul woke up from his stupor and sat up, annoyed by his son's yelling. He stood up and saw Michael with Sabean; Paul knew it was the wolfdog he had abandoned.

He grabbed a stick and yelled at Mike, "You get away from that animal, you stupid kid!"

Sabean stood her ground and snarled at the sight of Paul. Her back hair bristled, and she growled while Paul approached her.

"Get in the tent, you stupid kid," Paul yelled.

Mike pleaded, "Please don't hurt her."

Mike feared for Sabean but knew to obey his father and ran to the tent; Joyce opened the tent flap and grabbed Mike inside.

Paul approached Sabean with the stick held high. She bared her teeth, but her posture betrayed her cautiousness; her previous experiences taught her to fear this man. She regained courage and started to move toward Paul. The stick Paul held was long and sturdy. He began to wave it wildly while taunting Sabean with loud verbal abuse. As Paul moved back, he backed hard into the ravine warning sign; his pain enraged him. Paul turned and hit the sign hard, breaking the stick. Although smaller, Paul picked up another stick and advanced toward Sabean, waving the stick as he moved toward her.

Instantaneously Sabean's pack ran out from the bush. They formed a half-moon around Paul. Paul's confidence died, and he slowly backed up again. Tembah snarled at him, showing his dangerous teeth. Paul went further back at the sight of the wolves. As he stepped back near the ravine's edge, he must have felt the earth crumble beneath his feet, but it was too late for Paul to move ahead. He fell backward headfirst down the ravine. Paul flung out his arms, trying to grab at something to save himself, but without success. He howled in pain and yelled something no one could understand as he fell to his death. Paul's neck and body landed on the bottom of the ravine with an eerie splash and thud.

Joyce had squeezed her eyes shut at the sound of Paul's screams but opened them when they stopped. She held Michael tightly inside the tent and watched through the tent flap. Sabean and her pack ran off down a path and disappeared.

Joyce waited a bit, then kneeled at Mike's eye level and said, "Please listen to me carefully, Michael. I need you to stay inside the tent until I call you."

Michael obeyed without a word. Joyce unzipped the tent door and ventured over to where Paul had fallen. Shocked, Joyce stared at Paul, not knowing what to do. She turned to check Michael and saw him peeking through the tent flap.

"Michael William Ross, stay inside the tent!" Joyce yelled, and Mike complied.

Bill and Alfie heard Paul's screams and ran toward the sound. It wasn't long before the two men appeared with wide eyes behind Joyce.

"What happened here?" Alfred asked.

Joyce slowly turned toward the men shaking her head in disbelief.

"Come away now; let us help you back to your tent. Do you have a cell phone?" Bill asked. Joyce tried her phone but couldn't get reception.

"Alfred, go to the cabin, get the phone key, call the police, and tell them we need an ambulance," Bill instructed.

"Okay," Alfred responded.

"Please sit down in the chair until the authorities arrive," Bill helped Joyce back to her tent and into the chair. He saw multiple bruises on the woman's arms.

"We'll stay with you until you feel a little calmer; we won't leave you, Joyce," Bill consoled.

"How do you know my name?" She asked. "I'm Bill, we've met before, and you served me ice tea," He affirmed.

"I remember you, Bill. Joyce looked up, "My Lord has sent me a Christian." Thank you for helping us." Joyce voiced.

Hearing the boy crying, Bill asked, "Is that your son inside the tent?"

"Yes, he's distraught," Joyce answered.

"Would you mind if I ask him to come out? I think he needs his mom," Bill ventured.

"Yes, you're right, Michael; you can come out now, dear," Joyce said.

Mike came out, and Joyce embraced her son.

Joyce was still shaking from the unnerving episode and pointed to the ravine.

She said, "That's my husband, Paul. He told Michael to get away from the animal. I saw him move backward when more wolves appeared and moved toward him, unafraid of Paul.

Joyce explained He was very drunk and backed up too far and fell.

"Wolves," Bill queried.

"Well, the first animal looked like a wolfdog we lost; she was a wolf and shepherd cross, and we called her Sabean. She ran away some time ago. Paul seemed to be handling himself until the other wolves joined her," Joyce explained.

"It was Sabean, mom. Please don't hurt her, mister. Do you think the police will kill her?" Michael said, still shaking a bit.

Sadly, it was clear it was Sabean and not his father in Michael's mind and heart.

"Wait a minute; I know that wolfdog and her family. They have never bothered us and keep to themselves. It was my first time seeing her and her family in the campground area. Something must have riled them. Bill remarked.

Joyce interjected and explained what she thought might have happened. Her face was filled with compassion as she hugged Mike with tears running down her face.

Joyce surmised, "I think her family was protecting her. Paul was threatening her, and then the wolves came out of the bushes."

Alfred returned and said he had notified the police and the ambulance.

"What do you think, Joyce? Should we mention your wolfdog and her family? Did they knock your husband down the ravine," Bill inquired.

"No, I think they were just trying to save Sabean from Paul's advances," Joyce conveyed,

"Let's not mention the animals. I can't take any more violence; I just want to rest somewhere away from here."

"I'm afraid we have to stick around until the police arrive, but you can take as much time as you need at our place next door when they go," Bill suggested.

It was four in the afternoon before the police arrived. Officer Grant Colwell walked down the path to the campsite and joined them.

"Can you tell me what happened?" asked Grant while staring at Joyce's bruised arms.

Still in shock, Joyce explained she was inside the tent and unsure of what had happened. All I could do was hold onto my son as I heard Paul's screams,"

Sirens howled from the ambulance upon arrival.

Alfie walked over to the EMTs and led them to the accident site. One attendant looked down to inspect the body and announced that it looked like Paul had a broken neck by the position of his head. Carefully backing the ambulance near the ravine side, they lowered a stretcher down the ravine while the other attendant roped himself down to where Paul lay. The attendant buckled Paul onto the stretcher and yelled, "Ready!" The other attendant on top hit the button on the ambulance, and Paul's body made its way up, with the other attendant following close behind on the rope. They loaded the body into the ambulance. The larger of the two EMTs walked over to the police and Joyce and told them that he was taking Paul to the mortuary at the hospital and then drove away.

Officer Colwell questioned Joyce and said she could return to town with him if she felt she couldn't drive. Bill and Alfie told Grant they would stay with her until she felt up to it. The policeman said he was sorry for her loss and proceeded down the path to his cruiser.

Joyce was full of confusing feelings, and deep down, she couldn't help but feel somewhat relieved that it wasn't Mike that fell. Bill and Al packed the tent and camping materials and put them in the back of the truck.

"Are you going to be okay?" Bill asked.

"I'm a bit better now, but I'd like to sit at your place for a while.

The four of them walked to the cabin. Joyce climbed the stairs and immediately sat down on the rocker. Michael took his place on the stairs

"Joyce, I will make you some herb tea to soothe your nerves if that's okay with you," Bill offered.

"That might help. You both have gone out of your way for my son and me. I surely appreciate it." Joyce expressed.

Bill told Michael, "So her name is Sabean, eh? I never knew what to call her. She comes by herself to visit us and mooch any food available. However, she seldom comes since she met her mate, the big black wolf, and I miss her. The other wolves you saw, Joyce, must have been her offspring. I'm glad she isn't alone anymore." Bill added, "If you like, we'll get your phone number, and if she starts to visit again more often, we'll let you know. Please feel free to come and visit us anytime you like."

"That's very kind of you, thank you," Joyce answered. "Yes, thank you, Mr. Dennis. I would love to see Sabean again." Michael added.

An hour or two later, and a couple of Bill's teas, Joyce said she felt ready to drive home.

"Thank you again for all your help," Joyce said as she and Mike got into the truck.

Looking back for a moment, Joyce finally turned the key and drove onto the road. As she drove down the hill, the sun was going down.

Sabean and her pack stood on a hill overlooking the road. As Joyce's truck passed by, the pack howled a haunting chorus. Mike, hearing the howls, said he believed Sabean and her family were saying goodbye to them; Joyce agreed.

In the distance, the Rocky Hill pack began to howl, too. Bill and Alfred enjoyed hearing the howls. They folded their hands and prayed for Joyce and her son.

And now, much has been lost for Joyce and Michael, but much still is theirs, for the Good Shepherd, Jesus, is with them. He will go before them and safely guide their way into the future.

Isaiah 49:16a

Even these may forget, yet I will not forget you. Behold, I have engraved you on the palms of my hands.

THE END

Linda Bondy at PageMaster's store
https://pagemasterpublishing.ca/by/linda-bondy/

To order more copies of this book, find books by other
Canadian authors, or make inquiries about publishing your
own book, contact PageMaster at:

PageMaster Publication Services Inc.
11340-120 Street, Edmonton, AB T5G 0W5
books@pagemaster.ca
780-425-9303

catalogue and e-commerce store
PageMasterPublishing.ca/Shop